A NEW WINDMILL BOOK OF SHORT STORIES

TALES IN THE TELLING

Heinemann
New Windmills

Heinemann Educational Publishers
Halley Court, Jordan Hill, Oxford OX2 8EJ
A division of Reed Educational and Professional Publishing Ltd

OXFORD MELBOURNE AUCKLAND
JOHANNESBURG BLANTYRE GABORONE
IBADAN PORTSMOUTH (NH) USA CHICAGO

04 03 02 01
10 9 8 7 6 5 4 3 2

ISBN 0 435 125222

Acknowledgements

The Editor and Publishers would like to thank the following for permission to use
copyright material: Curtis Brown Ltd., New York, on behalf of Jane Yolen for 'Momster in the
Closet' from *Bruce Colville's Book of Monsters*, published by Scholastic, Inc. Copyright © 1993
by Jane Yolen; Oxford University Press, Australia, for 'Incident at Dusk' by Claudia Baharini from
Splinters, edited by Richard Baines. Copyright © Oxford University Press, Australia and New
Zealand; David Higham Associates Ltd. on behalf of Langston Hughes for 'Thank you M'am';
Sternig & Byrne Literary Agency on behalf of the Estate of Jack Ritchie for 'Shatter Proof',
originally published in 'Manhunt' October, 1960; Penguin Books Ltd. for 'Woman and Home' by
Robert Westall from *The Call and Other Stories* by Robert Westall, (Viking 1989). Copyright ©
1989 by Robert Westall; Sheil Land Associates Ltd. on behalf of Susan Hill for 'Farthing House'
Copyright © 1992 by Susan Hill; Peters Fraser & Dunlop Group Ltd. on behalf of the Estate of
Frank O'Connor for 'My Oedipus Complex'; Ann Walsh for 'Getting Away From It All' from *The
Skin of the Soul*; Doubleday, a Division of Random House Inc., on behalf of Isaac Asimov for
'Star Light' from *Isaac Asimov: The Complete Stories vol 2* Copyright © 1962 by Hoffman
Electronics Corporation; David Higham Associates Ltd. on behalf of Arthur C. Clarke for
'Reunion' from *The Wind from the Sun*, Copyright © 1972 by Arthur C. Clarke; Jonathan Clowes
Ltd. on behalf of Doris Lessing for 'Through the Tunnel' from *The Habit of Loving* by Doris
Lessing, Copyright © 1954 by Doris Lessing; Penguin Books Ltd. for 'The Angel of the Central
Line' by Nina Bawden from *Just in Time: Stories to Mark the Millennium* (Puffin 1999).
Copyright © 1999 by Nina Bawden; The Barbara Hogenson Agency, Inc. New York, on behalf of
the Estate of James Thurber for 'The Secret Life of Walter Mitty' from *My World – And Welcome
to it* by James Thurber. Copyright © 1942 by James Thurber, renewed 1971 by Helen Thurber
and Rosemary A. Thurber. Reprinted by arrangement with Rosemary A. Thurber.

Whilst every effort has been made to locate the owners of copyright, in some cases this has
been unsuccessful. The publishers apologise for any infringement or failure to acknowledge the
original sources and will be glad to include any necessary correction in subsequent printings.

Cover design by The Point

Cover illustration by Mark Shattoch

Illustrations by Jackie Hill at 320 Design; 'Thank you M'am' – Hashim Akib; 'The Examination
Result' – Philip Bannister; 'Shatter Proof' – Claudio Muñoz; 'The Sweet Old Lady Who Cried
Wolf' – Hashim Akib; 'Woman and Home' – Neil Parker; 'Farthing House' – David Hopkins; 'My
Oedipus Complex' – Paul Cemmick; 'Star Light' – Hashim Akib; 'Through the Tunnel' – Philip
Bannister; 'The Angel of the Central Line' – Hashim Akib; 'The Secret Life of Walter Mitty' – Paul
Cemmick.
Typeset by Tek-Art, Croydon, Surrey
Printed and bound in the United Kingdom by Clays Ltd, St Ives plc

Contents

Introduction for Students

The main aim of this collection is variety. It contains 17 short (including some *very* short) stories on different subjects, told in a wide range of different ways. Some are funny, some serious; some have been written recently, some are a bit older. None of them is dull. Many have unpredictable plots with a twist at the end.

The title, **Tales in the Telling**, needs a word of explanation. The National Curriculum for Key Stage 3 says that you should learn more about how stories *work*: that is, about the way they are told. You have to understand *how* writers build up their plots, present their characters, create settings and use different viewpoints to hold your interest. The activities at the back of the book are there to help you do just that.

You also need to be familiar with the *types* of story that are written. These are known as 'genres' – Thrillers, Crime and Detection, Romance, Science Fiction, Mystery Stories, and so on. What marks out one genre from another? Why do writers choose a particular genre? How should youread them? This book will support you in finding your own answers.

Apart from the last one, the stories are grouped in pairs. This is partly to give the book a clear shape. It is also because you can sometimes get more out of one story by comparing it with another which is in some ways similar. However, the stories do not *have* to be read in twos. I've chosen them because they are all good enough to be read in their own right. See if you agree.

Mike Royston

Introduction for Teachers

The stories in this collection focus attention on the chief elements of narrative technique: plot structure and development, characterization, style and language, the creation of setting and atmosphere and varieties of viewpoint. The intention is to help students consider 'what makes a good story?' and to appreciate that short fictions are consciously crafted by writers who make careful *choices* about the best way to tell them.

The selection of stories has been determined, first and foremost, by their intrinsic appeal to teenage readers. All have been recently trialled with students across the age and ability range of Key Stage 3. They include seven which are specified in QCA's Draft Scheme of Work on Short Stories for KS3 (2000), namely: *Farthing House, My Oedipus Complex, Getting Away From It All, Reunion, The Doll's House, Through the Tunnel* and *The Secret Life of Walter Mitty.*

The activities at the back of this book encourage a comparative approach to study, though they also allow for detailed examination of single stories through pair-, group- and whole class work. Equally important, students are helped to create their own narratives with, it is hoped, an enhanced awareness of how to guide and control a reader's response.

Mike Royston

Momster in the Closet
Jane Yolen

'There's a momster in my closet,' Kenny said. 'I heard him this morning.'

'Grumpf ouff,' Dad said, his mouth full.

'That's nice, dear. Do you want some more?' Mom asked.

You see, with Kenny it was something new in that closet every day. At five – 'And a half!' he'd be quick to remind you – he had more imagination than sense. Also, he watched too much TV.

'Come on, squirt,' I said, 'or we'll be late.' I took an extra-long swallow as Kenny shrugged into his backpack. He followed me out of the door.

'Was, too, a momster,' he said.

'Monster,' I corrected automatically.

'With long grungy hair. And weird claws. He was nine feet . . . no, ten feet tall.'

'Heard all that through the door?' I asked.

That shut him up. Of course, last week it had been a weirdwolf. The time before it had been a ghould. He didn't know how to pronounce the stuff, but he was convinced they were all there. That must be *some* closet, I thought, and said so out loud.

'Right to Momster Land,' Kenny said.

Kids! I could hardly recall ever being that young. It felt as if I had been a teenager forever.

When we got home, the sun was sitting just below the horizon. Summers are hard around here. There is just not enough night.

'Come on, squirt,' I said. 'Time for bed.'

'I don't want to go,' Kenny said. 'There's a momster in the closet.'

'You have to. I have to. That's the way of the world,' I said. 'Besides, it's monster. Spelled with an *n* not an *m*.'

'It's got spells, too?' Kenny said. 'Oh, no – it will *really* get me.'

'There's nothing there,' I said, my patience beginning to go. 'Besides, if it threatens you, just growl back at it and show your teeth like this.' I bared my fangs at him.

Kenny giggled.

We went inside. Mom had already settled down, but Dad was still up, sitting in front of the TV and watching the flag flapping in time to the National Anthem. It's only a little more exciting than a test pattern. He didn't seem to hear us.

Kenny and I went into the room we shared, and I helped him get undressed. He still has trouble with the knots in his shoelaces. I keep asking Mom to find him a pair of Velcro sneakers.

Once we were in our pyjamas and had brushed our teeth, he raced ahead of me to his bed. He turned for a moment and growled at the closet.

'Fangs for the memory,' I said.

He giggled again, though I don't think he got the joke.

'Last one in is a . . .' he shouted.

'. . . rotten . . .' I prompted.

'corpse!' He made a funny face and lay down. Once his eyes were closed, he was very still.

I kissed his forehead, moving aside the hair as white-gold as corn silk, and tenderly closed the lid over him. Then I climbed into my own coffin, pulling it shut before the first light of day could come streaming through the blinds. Monsters in the closet, indeed! Kenny knew, as I did, that only sunlight or a stake through the heart can really kill a vampire.

I closed my eyes and slept.

Incident at Dusk
Claudia Baharini

We came up onto the high plains as dusk was falling. The plains were as flat as pressed sand though all I could see in the failing light was the **dun** colour of scorched treebark. It was quiet on the plains and there was no wind stirring. We kept a strict formation, one man behind the other, as we had been instructed to do in the camps.

Immediately ahead of me was Gub, my old friend from training days at the base. I kept a close watch on him as we trekked across the open spaces, his shape moving in a series of jerks like a figure lit by lightning.

It was dangerous to venture out before nightfall, but times were difficult and we had been forced to break our normal routine.

'Hold!'

The line came to a sudden halt, and I dug in my feet to avoid running into Gub. We stood there nervously for perhaps a full minute listening to the hollow sound of silence all around us and wondering what had caught the Commander's attention. The darkness was thickening now, and only a thin halo of twilight hovered across the plain. I strained my eyes and peered into the gloom, wondering if it was time to switch on the sensors. No order had been given, so I just continued to stare.

'**Sinister, thirty**.'

I gazed across the darkening plateau. Nothing there, I thought. We knew the plateau ran for miles before falling sharply away in a smooth scree to the valley below.

---

dun: dark

sinister, thirty: a military command, instructing the men to look 30 degrees to their left

We had strict orders not to approach the scree. It formed the border of our territory. No one I knew had ever approached the scree and returned to base camp to tell of it. Beyond the scree was Namuh, an empty wasteland that throbbed with unchartered sounds and strange mystic lights that filled us all with terror and dread.

And then I saw it. Gub must have sensed it at the same time as I did, for I noticed him stiffen and his head jerk upwards as if a nerve had been touched at the top of his spine.

'Over there,' he whispered in a throaty gasp, and then, 'What can it be?'

The object was circular, standing to our left and looking like a gigantic saucer. It was clearly a ship from Namuh and the Outer Reaches.

'I have never seen such a thing.'

It was huge. Above its plate-like base sat a series of circular humps and domes, each one rising above the next in a pattern of architectural ripples. In the sullen gloom I could just detect a twinge of colour about them, orange, red and green. It was a fearsome structure, towering above us and merging with the grey of the gathering skies. As we stood trembling on the open prairie the Commander gave the order for us to switch on the sensors. Immediately a warm glow flooded through my being, and, as I adjusted my antennae, I could taste a distinctively vegetable tang in the air.

'I do not understand.'

Gub was as terrified as I was. Now that the sensors were operating fully I could pick up the tension and panic reaching me from the lines of foragers spread out across the plain.

'We must go back.'

We were frightened, but we had been well trained. No one moved. Standing there we tried desperately to register any signs of life from the large space ship beside us. It was active, that we could tell, reeking of living matter, but there was no movement on it. So we waited, frozen to the hard earth, sensing the enormous life-force that loomed above us; and the ship from the Outer Reaches, silent and motionless, watched us in return.

The Commander then made a fatal decision. Looking back I can understand it. Times were hard and our larders were empty. We had become desperate. But from the moment I heard the order to advance I knew we were courting disaster.

I picked up Gub's wry grin on the sensor, and he, no doubt, sensed my alarm. There was nothing else we could do. The lines shuffled into action, moving like boxcars. We increased our speed. We had only advanced several paces when our world exploded.

It started with a blinding flash of light, brighter than many suns burning down upon us from the stratosphere. The first thing it did was to throw our sensors into disarray, driving the vapours from our heads and fusing the screens. Spots and shadows danced in my brain as I tried desperately to focus my eyes. Then, amidst the noise of thunder and gunfire, a Creature larger than the plain, larger than the foreign ship, larger even than the screes of Namuh burst through the firmament.

The Creature walked in the chasm, faded into the grey mists of space and time, loomed above us.

I stood frozen in fear.

As the winds howled around our ears and the lights flickered in my head I tasted bile in my throat and smelt the sour odour of acid across the plain.

I looked up at Gub and saw panic in the mosaic of his eyes before he was whisked off the plateau even as I stared. He and a hundred others were caught up in a flurry of whistling winds and sweeping storms and removed in a single action from my cosy world. As it was, the force of the blow lifted me off my feet and slammed me against the hard surface of the burnt earth, knocking me unconscious.

When I awoke I was lying on the edge of the precipice above the scree. Below me was the void. I have never in my life seen anything as frightening as that dark gaseous eye that stared up unblinking into mine. I realised that I was gazing into the dead heart of Namuh. I do not know how long I lay in that position before I managed to tear myself away from the sheer drop in front of me. In the same instant I saw to my horror that I was the sole survivor of our doomed expedition.

'I always enjoy an apple at bedtime.'

A solitary ant made his slow way back across the kitchen benchtop.

Thank You, M'am

Langston Hughes

She was a large woman with a large **purse** that had everything in it but a hammer and nails. It had a long strap, and she carried it slung across her shoulder. It was about eleven o'clock at night, dark, and she was walking alone, when a boy ran up behind her and tried to snatch her purse. The strap broke with the sudden single tug the boy gave it from behind. But the boy's weight and the weight of the purse combined caused him to lose his balance. Instead of taking off full blast as he had hoped, the boy fell on his back on the sidewalk and his legs flew up. The large woman simply turned around and kicked him right square in his blue-jeaned sitter. Then she reached down, picked the boy up by his shirt front, and shook him until his teeth rattled.

After that the woman said, 'Pick up my **pocketbook**, boy, and give it here.'

She still held him tightly. But she bent down enough to permit him to stoop and pick up her purse. Then she said, 'Now ain't you ashamed of yourself?'

Firmly gripped by his shirt front, the boy said, 'Yes'm.'

The woman said, 'What did you want to do it for?'

The boy said, 'I didn't aim to.'

She said, 'You a lie!'

By that time two or three people passed, stopped, turned to look, and some stood watching.

'If I turn you loose, will you run?' asked the woman.

'Yes'm,' said the boy.

---

purse: handbag

pocketbook: a more old-fashioned word for handbag

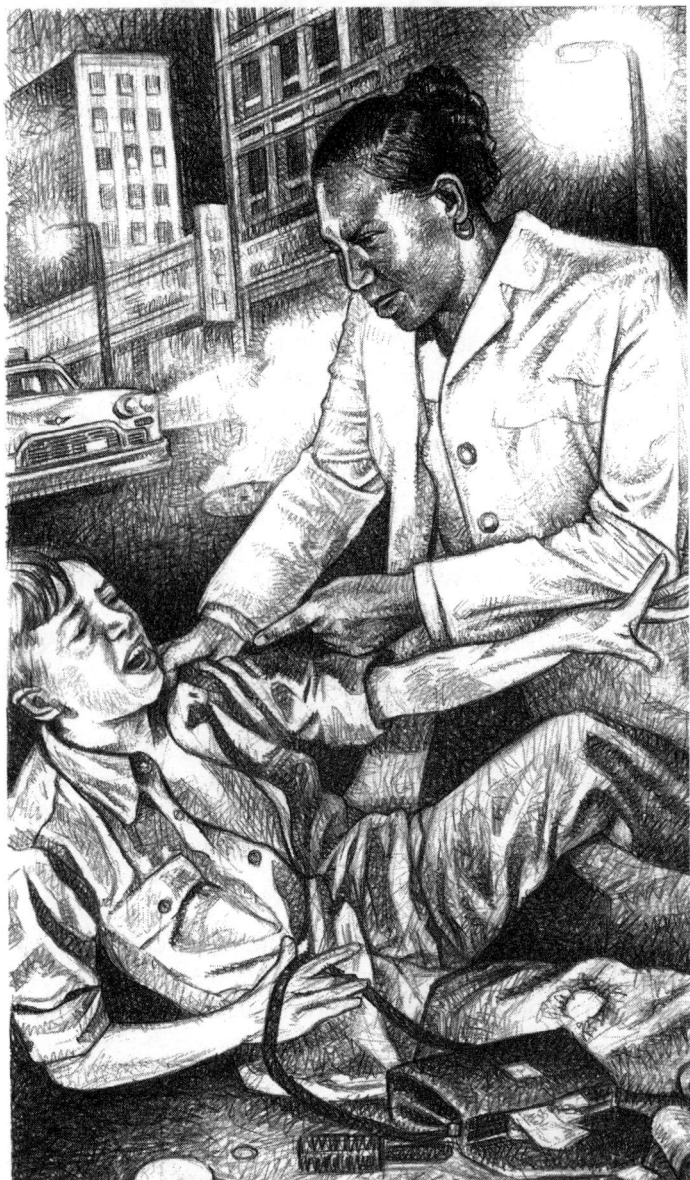

'Then I won't turn you loose,' said the woman. She did not release him.

'Lady, I'm sorry,' whispered the boy.

'Um-hum! Your face is dirty. I got a great mind to wash your face for you. Ain't you got nobody home to tell you to wash your face?'

'No'm,' said the boy.

'Then it will get washed this evening,' said the large woman, starting up the street, dragging the frightened boy behind her.

He looked as if he were fourteen or fifteen, frail and willow-wild, in tennis shoes and blue jeans.

The woman said, 'You ought to be my son. I would teach you right from wrong. Least I can do right now is to wash your face. Are you hungry?'

'No'm,' said the being-dragged boy. 'I just want you to turn me loose.'

'Was I bothering *you* when I turned that corner?' asked the woman.

'No'm.'

'But you put yourself in contact with *me*,' said the woman. 'If you think that contact is not going to last a while, you got another thought coming. When I get through with you, sir, you are going to remember Mrs Luella Bates Washington Jones.'

Sweat popped out on the boy's face and he began to struggle. Mrs Jones stopped, jerked him around in front of her, put a **half nelson** about his neck, and continued to drag him up the street. When she got to her door, she dragged the boy inside, down a hall, and into a large kitchenette-furnished room at the rear of the house. She switched on the light and left the door open. The boy could hear other roomers laughing and talking in the large house. Some of their doors were open, too, so he

---

half nelson: a hold in wrestling

knew he and the woman were not alone. The woman still had him by the neck in the middle of her room.

She said, 'What is your name?'

'Roger,' answered the boy.

'Then, Roger, you go to that sink and wash your face,' said the woman, whereupon she turned him loose – at last. Roger looked at the door – looked at the woman – looked at the door – *and went to the sink*.

'Let the water run until it gets warm,' she said. 'Here's a clean towel.'

'You gonna take me to jail?' asked the boy, bending over the sink.

'Not with that face, I would not take you nowhere,' said the woman. 'Here I am trying to get home to cook me a bite to eat, and you snatch my pocketbook! Maybe you ain't been to your supper either, late as it be. Have you?'

'There's nobody home at my house,' said the boy.

'Then we'll eat,' said the woman. 'I believe you're hungry – or been hungry – to try to snatch my pocketbook!'

'I want a pair of blue suede shoes,' said the boy.

'Well, you didn't have to snatch *my* pocketbook to get some suede shoes,' said Mrs Luella Bates Washington Jones. 'You could of asked me.'

'M'am?'

The water dripping from his face, the boy looked at her. There was a long pause. A very long pause. After he had dried his face, and not knowing what else to do, dried it again, the boy turned around, wondering what next. The door was open. He could make a dash for it down the hall. He could run, run, run, *run!*

The woman was sitting on the daybed. After a while she said, 'I were young once and I wanted things I could not get.'

There was another long pause. The boy's mouth opened. Then he frowned, not knowing he frowned.

The woman said, 'Um-hum! You thought I was going to say *but*, didn't you? You thought I was going to say, *but I didn't snatch people's pocketbooks*. Well, I wasn't going to say that.' Pause. Silence. 'I have done things, too, which I would not tell you, son – neither tell God, if He didn't already know. Everybody's got something in common. So you set down while I fix us something to eat. You might run that comb through your hair so you will look presentable.'

In another corner of the room behind a screen was a gas plate and an icebox. Mrs Jones got up and went behind the screen. The woman did not watch the boy to see if he was going to run now, nor did she watch her purse, which she left behind her on the daybed. But the boy took care to sit on the far side of the room, away from the purse, where he thought she could easily see him out of the corner of her eye if she wanted to. He did not trust the woman *not* to trust him. And he did not want to be mistrusted now.

'Do you need somebody to go to the store,' asked the boy, 'maybe to get some milk or something?'

'Don't believe I do,' said the woman, 'unless you just want sweet milk yourself. I was going to make some cocoa out of this canned milk I got here.'

'That will be fine,' said the boy.

She heated some lima beans and ham she had in the icebox, made the cocoa, and set the table. The woman did not ask the boy anything about where he lived, or his folks, or anything else that would embarrass him. Instead, as they ate, she told him about her job in a hotel beauty shop that stayed open late, what the work was like, and how all kinds of women came in and out, blonds, redheads, and Spanish. Then she cut him a half of her ten-cent cake.

'Eat some more, son,' she said.

When they were finished eating, she got up and said, 'Now here, take this ten dollars and buy yourself some blue suede shoes. And next time, do not make the mistake of latching onto *my* pocketbook *nor nobody else's* – because shoes got by devilish ways will burn your feet. I got to get my rest now. But from here on in, son, I hope you will behave yourself.'

She led him down the hall to the front door and opened it. 'Goodnight! Behave yourself, boy!' she said, looking out into the street as he went down the steps.

The boy wanted to say something other than, 'Thank you, M'am,' to Mrs Luella Bates Washington Jones, but although his lips moved, he couldn't even say that as he turned at the foot of the barren stoop and looked up at the large woman in her door. Then she shut the door.

Figurative language

- Poetic
- not straight forward + factual
- Imagery
- suggests more than meets the eye.

Imagery - interesting, gives more depth provides more for readers imagination without overdoing.

Metaphor

The sun is a yellow balloon

Simili

the sun is like a yellow balloon

The Examination Result
Alun Williams

Happened about <u>thirty</u> years ago. I was <u>eleven</u>. We were just the five brothers at home: Cornelius, Emlyn, Emrys, Edwin and myself. My mother had died when I was two and I remembered nothing of her. There was no photograph of her in the house. My father, during the three years he survived, had destroyed them all to blunt the stab of recollection.

Cornelius had started a small business and by means of working from dawn till midnight was doing quite well. Cornelius was a <u>very bright lad</u>. He had won a scholarship to the Grammar School, but had been unable to take it up because mother's illness ate up the money in the house and made my father ignore everything except her.

This fact had a curious effect on Cornelius. He saw it as the chief defeat of his life and he made sure that Emrys, Emlyn and Edwin won their scholarships and made their way to the Grammar School. But it was on me that he centred his greatest hopes. He said that we four would blaze a trail of glory through the Grammar School with me providing the brightest flames at the rear, the last and best.

Each evening after work or at slack periods during the hours when I helped him in the shop he checked on the state of my English and arithmetic. He bought me a little library of good books and saw that I read them. 'I'm willing to work in that shop,' he would say. '<u>For you</u> I would work right through the night, clean the floor of the potato shed with my own body, but don't let me down, any of you. That's all I ask.' His eyes would settle, green and intense, on me. '<u>You especially</u>.'

And so we came to the spring of the year in which I was to sit the scholarship examination for Grammar School.

The golden weather came soon that year and Cornelius kept me back from the lovely beckoning slopes on which I wanted to play with my friends.

'Time for that later,' he said. 'I do without things I want, a lot of things. So can you with a prize like that at stake.' I can still see the strain on his face as he said that. I heard later that he told the girl he was friendly with that he would not marry until I, the youngest of the brothers, had completed a course at the University, ten or eleven years to go. She said that she could not wait so long and left him.

I got wound up with anxiety a week before the examination. I had violent stomach cramp. At school I would sit without a word in the corner of the concrete-covered yard, not even lifting my head when my friends crowded round me and told me to stop being moody. I said nothing about this to Cornelius in case he might think I was making excuses in advance.

On the day of the examination, every inch of my body was in a turmoil. The pain got right into the nib and made it blunder foolishly. I made every mistake in arithmetic and spelling within reach. The exam was held in the art room of the Grammar School. The walls were hung with plaster casts of tigers' mouths and human lips, utterly silent and utterly threatening. As I left the room at the end of the afternoon, even the air through which I walked seemed to crumble in ruin.

It was on a Friday that our headmaster, Mr Robias, ordered the whole school to be brought into the main hall. He said that the school had had a triumph. We had twice as many pupils on the list as any other school in that area.

He read out the names. My senses picked up every speck of sensation as the loud, proud baritone voice boomed out its message. My name was not called.

I was first out of the hall. I ran alone on to the hillside that rose steeply behind the street in which I lived. I sat

down, my back tight against a small wild apple tree that had a hole in it into which my back fitted. It had been mine since early childhood. It was where I went whenever I felt too angry, lost or cheated. My eyes were fixed on the back of our house, on the kitchen door through which Cornelius would pass at a quarter to six when he came down for tea.

I grew hungry. When Cornelius came into sight and put his hand on the latch of the kitchen door it had the effect on me of a summons. I got up and made my way down to the house, my mind and heart empty of everything except my fear.

When I went in, my brothers were seated at the table, eating in silence. Not one of them looked up as I came in. I sat on my chair. There were pockets of silence in all four corners of the kitchen. I was excited by the sight of food but my fingers could not bring themselves to approach it.

'Well?' said Cornelius.

'I didn't pass,' I said. I wanted to run, but my legs had worked themselves round the legs of the chair and would not budge.

Cornelius stood up and threw his knife and fork on the plate with a terrifying clatter. He leaned over and hit my face with his full strength. The blow toppled me off the chair. I heard a few vague little sounds of protest from Emrys, Emlyn and Edwin. I shouted something angry, a formless childish oath that caught up a thousandth of the rage and bewilderment I felt.

Cornelius raised his arm again, but I slithered along the floor and shot my hand up to the latch of the door. The iron latch had been worn thin and sharp by age and use. I felt it cut my skin. But the door opened and out I rushed. No one followed.

Shatter Proof
Jack Ritchie

He was a soft-faced man wearing rimless glasses, but he handled the automatic with unmistakable competence.

I was rather surprised at my calmness when I learned the reason for his presence. 'It's a pity to die in ignorance,' I said. 'Who hired you to kill me?'

His voice was mild. 'I could be an enemy in my own right.'

I had been making a drink in my study when I had heard him and turned. Now I finished pouring from the decanter. 'I know the enemies I've made and you are a stranger. Was it my wife?'

He smiled. 'Quite correct. Her motive must be obvious.'

'Yes,' I said. 'I have money and apparently she wants it. All of it.'

He regarded me objectively. 'Your age is?'

'Fifty-three.'

'And your wife is?'

'Twenty-two.'

He clicked his tongue. 'You were foolish to expect anything permanent, Mr Williams.'

I sipped the whiskey. 'I expected a divorce after a year or two and a painful settlement. But not death.'

'Your wife is a beautiful woman, but greedy, Mr Williams. I'm surprised that you never noticed.'

My eyes went to the gun. 'I assume you have killed before?'

'Yes.'

'And obviously you enjoy it.'

He nodded. 'A morbid pleasure, I admit. But I do.'

I watched him and waited. Finally I said, 'You have been here more than two minutes and I am still alive.'

'There is no hurry, Mr Williams,' he said softly.

'Ah, then the actual killing is not your greatest joy. You must savor the preceding moments.'

'You have insight, Mr Williams.'

'And as long as I keep you entertained, in one manner or another, I remain alive?'

'Within a time limit, of course.'

'Naturally. A drink, Mr . . . ?'

'Smith requires no strain on the memory. Yes, thank you. But please allow me to see what you are doing when you prepare it.'

'It's hardly likely that I would have poison conveniently at hand for just such an occasion.'

'Hardly likely, but still possible.'

He watched me while I made his drink and then took an easy chair.

I sat on the **davenport**. 'Where would my wife be at this moment?'

'At a party, Mr Williams. There will be a dozen people to swear that she never left their sight during the time of your murder.'

'I will be shot by a burglar? An intruder?'

He put his drink on the cocktail table in front of him. 'Yes. After I shoot you, I shall, of course, wash this glass and return it to your liquor cabinet. And when I leave I shall wipe all fingerprints from the doorknobs I've touched.'

'You will take a few trifles with you? To make the burglar–intruder story more authentic?'

'That will not be necessary, Mr Williams. The police will assume that the burglar panicked after he killed you and fled empty-handed.'

'That picture on the east wall,' I said. 'It's worth thirty thousand.'

---

davenport: large sofa

His eyes went to it for a moment and then quickly returned to me. 'It is tempting, Mr Williams. But I desire to possess nothing that will even remotely link me to you. I appreciate art, and especially its monetary value, but not to the extent where I will risk the electric chair.' Then he smiled. 'Or were you perhaps offering me the painting? In exchange for your life?'

'It was a thought.'

He shook his head. 'I'm sorry, Mr Williams. Once I accept a **commission**, I am not dissuaded. It is a matter of professional pride.'

I put my drink on the table. 'Are you waiting for me to show fear, Mr Smith?'

'You will show it.'

'And then you will kill me?'

His eyes flickered. 'It's a strain, isn't it, Mr Williams? To be afraid and not to dare show it.'

'Do you expect your victims to beg?' I asked.

'They do. In one manner or another.'

'They appeal to your humanity. And that is hopeless?'

'It is hopeless.'

'They offer you money?'

'Very often.'

'Is that hopeless too?'

'So far it has been, Mr Williams.'

'Behind the picture I pointed out to you, Mr Smith, there is a wall safe.'

He gave the painting another brief glance. 'Yes.'

'It contains five thousand dollars.'

'That is a lot of money, Mr Williams.'

I picked up my glass and went to the painting. I opened the safe, selected a brown envelope, and then finished my drink. I put the empty glass in the safe and twirled the knob.

---

commission: contract to kill

Smith's eyes were drawn to the envelope. 'Bring that here, please.'

I put the envelope on the cocktail table in front of him.

He looked at it for a few moments and then up at me. 'Did you actually think you could buy your life?'

I lit a cigarette. 'No. You are, shall we say, incorruptible.'

He frowned slightly. 'But still you brought me the five thousand?'

I picked up the envelope and tapped its contents out on the table. 'Old receipts. All completely valueless to you.'

He showed the color of irritation. 'What do you think this has possibly gained you?'

'The opportunity to go to the safe and put your glass inside it.'

His eyes flicked to the glass in front of him. 'That was yours. Not mine.'

I smiled. 'It was your glass, Mr Smith. And I imagine that the police will wonder what an empty glass is doing in my safe. I rather think, especially since this will be a case of murder, that they will have the intelligence to take fingerprints.'

His eyes narrowed. 'I haven't taken my eyes off you for a moment. You couldn't have switched our glasses.'

'No? I seem to recall that at least twice you looked at the painting.'

Automatically he looked in that direction again. 'Only for a second or two.'

'It was enough.'

He was perspiring faintly. 'I say it was impossible.'

'Then I'm afraid you will be greatly surprised when the police come for you. And after a little while you will have the delightful opportunity of facing death in the electric chair. You will share your victim's anticipation of death with the addition of a great deal more time in which to let your imagination play with the topic. I'm sure you've read accounts of executions in the electric chair?'

His finger seemed to tighten on the trigger.

'I wonder how you'll go,' I said. 'You've probably pictured yourself meeting death with calmness and fortitude. But that is a common comforting delusion, Mr Smith. You will more likely have to be dragged . . .'

His voice was level. 'Open that safe or I'll kill you.'

I laughed. 'Really now, Mr Smith, we both know that obviously you will kill me if I *do* open the safe.'

A half a minute went by before he spoke. 'What do you intend to do with the glass?'

'If you don't murder me – and I rather think you won't now – I will take it to a private detective agency and have your fingerprints reproduced. I will put them, along with a note containing pertinent information, inside a sealed envelope. And I will leave instructions that in the event I die violently, even if the occurrence appears accidental, the envelope be forwarded to the police.'

Smith stared at me and then he took a breath. 'All that won't be necessary. I will leave now and you will never see me again.'

I shook my head. 'I prefer my plan. It provides protection for my future.'

He was thoughtful. 'Why don't you go direct to the police?'

'I have my reasons.'

His eyes went down to his gun and then slowly he put it in his pocket. An idea came to him. 'Your wife could very easily hire someone else to kill you.'

'Yes. She could do that.'

'I would be accused of your death. I could go to the electric chair.'

'I imagine so. Unless . . .'

Smith waited.

'Unless, of course, she were unable to hire anyone.'

'But there are probably half a dozen other . . .' He stopped.

I smiled. 'Did my wife tell you where she is now?'

'Just that she'd be at a place called the Petersons. She will leave at eleven.'

'Eleven? A good time. It will be very dark tonight. Do you know the Petersons' address?'

He stared at me. 'No.'

'In Bridgehampton,' I said, and I gave him the house number.

Our eyes held for half a minute.

'It's something you must do,' I said softly. 'For your own protection.'

He buttoned his coat slowly. 'And where will you be at eleven, Mr Williams?'

'At my club, probably playing cards with five or six friends. They will no doubt commiserate with me when I receive word that my wife has been . . . shot?'

'It all depends on the circumstances and the opportunity.' He smiled thinly. 'Did you ever love her?'

I picked up a jade figurine and examined it. 'I was extremely fond of this piece when I first bought it. Now it bores me. I will replace it with another.'

When he was gone there was just enough time to take the glass to a detective agency before I went on to the club.

Not the glass in the safe, of course. It held nothing but my own fingerprints.

I took the one that Mr Smith left on the cocktail table when he departed.

The prints of Mr Smith's fingers developed quite clearly.

The Sweet Old Lady Who Cried Wolf
Mari Waagaard

One day the sweet old lady came into the police station and said, 'Forgive my disturbing you again, Inspector, but you see, there's a dead body in my garden.'

She leaned confidentially across the desk and whispered, 'He's such a nice elderly gentleman. He's lying in my poppy bed in such a peculiar, twisted attitude. And there's a knife in his back too. I'm certain this must be foul play, Inspector; wilful and cold-blooded murder, don't you think?'

Chief Constable Ole **Gregersen** looked at Thea Dahl, his new assistant, and made a sign to her. Then he bent down and patted the sweet old lady on the arm and said reassuringly, 'Come now, Mrs Werle. Are you quite sure you saw a body? You may be mistaken, you know. Have another look. And promise me,' he pointed a mock-threatening finger, 'promise me you'll stop reading all that nonsense you're filling your pretty little head with. All those detective stories aren't good for you, you're much too sensitive and imaginative. Promise, Mrs Werle! Now, you be a good girl . . .'

The sweet old lady blushed, looked reproachfully at the policeman and muttered under her breath as she turned to leave the station, 'My, oh my, Inspector, you're incorrigible – and a great tease too. But I'll do as I'm told. I'll walk straight home and have another look. But I'm sure the gentleman with the knife will still be there. It's a shame. Anyway . . . Good day to you, Inspector, and to you too, Miss.'

Gregersen: this story is set in Oslo, the capital of Norway

Thea Dahl gazed appalled at her superior. 'For heaven's sake, Mr Gregersen, what if the woman's telling the truth? There *might* be a dead man in her garden. You really shouldn't snub her like that, Sir, a sweet old lady like her!'

Mr Gregersen grinned then sighed and said musingly, 'You're new here. If you weren't, you'd know that this little old lady, Agnete Werle, pops in every month or so to report crimes. Crimes which only exist in her imagination, that is. A murder, a theft, a swindle. You remember when Edward Munch's "Vampire" was stolen from the Munch Museum? She turned up regularly once a week and told us where we could find the painting. It was even hanging in her sitting-room! As we didn't know her then we sent a couple of the boys to check, just in case, but of course it was sheer nonsense. Actually we checked false reports of thefts and murders on several occasions and gave her quite a talking-to. She just looked at us with those innocent blue eyes and said she was sorry! She is very sweet but more than a bit eccentric and I think a little bit soft in the head too. But don't worry, I won't offend her or hurt her. After all, she wouldn't hurt a fly.'

Gregersen paused and thought for a while, then went on, 'I feel sorry for her, in a way, although she seems happy enough. She's rich, mind you – rolling in money and she lives in a beautiful house, all inherited from her husband. He was a war hero – fought in the resistance against the Nazis.'

Thea Dahl listened attentively. 'Does she really live by herself? She must be quite an age.'

'As a matter of fact she's in her eighties but she's fit as a fiddle. Alone, yes, but there's a woman who comes in to clean the house once a week and I think she rents out a room to a female student just to have a young person around, not for the cash of course; and she certainly is generous with her money . . .'

Meanwhile the young tenant in Mrs Werle's house, Ellida Wang, was deep in conversation with her boyfriend, Jorgen. Both 'students', both unemployed, both very broke, both obsessed with the idea of getting hold of money, lots of money, in the easiest way possible. They had tried burglary and the like without success and had so far avoided the police.

But now there was a chance of realising their dreams. Money, exciting journeys, *la dolce vita* . . . Let us listen for a moment to their interesting conversation.

Jorgen: To hell with your crappy sentimentality. It's settled now. The old bat has absolutely no use for all that cash. Damn Amnesty or Save the Children or whatever she gives it to. It's you and me who need to be saved – before we die of boredom and poverty.

Ellida: Okay, okay. But I can't help feeling a bit sorry for the old girl. I mean, she is very sweet in a way. And she relies on me. She's even told me she'll give me some money when I've graduated.

Jorgen: Shut up, idiot! When did you manage to pass an exam in your life? No, we've got to do the job. Remember, she's worth two million. It'll be like taking a lollipop from a baby.

Ellida: She's cleverer than you think, hides her dough pretty cunningly . . . Hey, look out of the window! Here she comes, toddling along. Look at her smile and that white hair – and look at that crazy hat!

Jorgen: Don't go all soft on her now. You weren't all that soft when we did over that old couple, remember? You laughed your head off when that old bloke saw his pension disappear . . . Well, I'd better make myself scarce before the old lady catches me.

Ellida was sitting with Ibsen's *The Doll's House* propped in front of her when Mrs Werle entered, flushed and breathless after her quick walk.

She beamed when she saw Ellida studying so diligently in the huge library.

'That's right, my dear. I see you're working hard and using my library as I told you to do. You'll find all the books you'll need here, classics and the moderns. But isn't it time you were off, Ellida? It's Wednesday: there's that lecture in old Norwegian literature this afternoon, the one you told me about, remember?'

When the young woman was out of sight Mrs Werle went straight to one of the shelves. She pulled out a couple of books. Between Doyle's *A Study in Scarlet* and Chesterton's *The Innocence of Father Brown* was a small tape recorder neatly hidden away.

It *had* to succeed this time.

Agnete Werle sat down in her best chair, rewound the tape and listened. She heard it all. 'To hell with your crappy sentimentality . . . we've got to do the job . . . worth two million . . . like taking a lollipop from a baby.'

Mrs Werle listened very carefully. She didn't miss a word. Then she played the whole conversation from the beginning again.

Oh yes, oh yes, she said and nodded repeatedly.

Then she took out a book by one of her favourite writers, Patricia Highsmith. But she had not read more than a few pages of *The Talented Mr Ripley* when she lowered the book and began to hum softly.

She always did when she was planning something.

'Hi, Mrs Werle! I've come straight from the lecture and I hope you don't mind my friend, he's a student too. Jorgen, meet Mrs Werle. Mrs Werle, this is Jorgen Thomassen, my – er – fiancé.'

Agnete started. She must have dozed off in her best chair with the book lying in her lap. Fortunately she had hidden the little tape recorder. She looked at her visitors;

slim bodies dressed in almost similar sweaters, jeans and sneakers. Two quite good-looking youngsters if it hadn't been for that watchful greedy look on their faces – oh yes – even on Ellida's, that was quite obvious now.

She said slowly, 'Any friend of Ellida's is a friend of mine. Glad to meet you, young man. You go to medical school, is that so? You'll end up as a surgeon, then – and Ellida studies art and she'll be a teacher in grammar school. Oh, you'll be successful, the two of you! Have you got far in your studies, Mr Thomassen?'

'Just a year or two left. But call me Jorgen, please. Ellida's your good friend and – '

'We have grown quite close, that's right. But do sit down. I'll make you a meal. You young people must be hungry.'

The old lady went off towards the kitchen, beaming and talking. 'I'll make you a really nice snack. Tea and sandwiches – relax, both of you! – make yourself at home, Jorgen, the way Ellida does. Oh, it's so lovely to have young people in the house.'

There was a pause. The boy and girl looked at each other. Jorgen tapped one finger against his head in a meaningful way.

'My young friends, I have a splendid idea!' Agnete almost ran into the sitting room again, clapping her hands in joy. 'Now listen. Ellida, I'm sure you remember that I've shown you all the rooms in the house *except* one. The secret room – the exciting room, Ellida!'

'Do you mean the bomb-proof room your husband built just before the second world war, is that the one?'

'Exactly, my dear,' cried Agnete, as if inspired. 'My husband had a very important and trusted position in the resistance movement during the German occupation. He was helping people escape to Sweden and Britain. That special room was so well hidden it was a marvellous place for anyone who had to hide from the Nazis, and for other

people too . . . It's under the cellar, beautifully furnished with a thick carpet on the floor and book shelves and expensive paintings – it's the most exciting, most bomb-proof and best secret room in Oslo, maybe in the whole of Norway! To show you how much I appreciate having you here I want us to celebrate in what is, for me, the most sacred room in the whole world. But now, I must finish in the kitchen. It won't take a minute.'

She disappeared again. Jorgen grinned at Ellida. He was holding a heavy silver candlestick in his hand, examining it.

Agnete reappeared out of breath, her cheeks rosy.

'Oh, I'm so looking forward to celebrating in there with you. Jorgen, you take this – oh, please don't fiddle with that candlestick, my cleaner isn't too fond of polishing silver and neither am I. By the way, there are two marvellous candelabra in the secret room, pure gold, you'll see. If you want something stronger than tea there's plenty to drink down there . . . Here we go. I'll lead the way.' Agnete smiled at them. She was all joy and enthusiasm.

'Watch it now, Ellida, here comes our chance,' whispered Jorgen as they followed the old lady down the cellar stairs and beyond, along the corridor lit by a faint bulb in the ceiling.

Eventually Agnete stopped in front of a massive half-open door. She turned to the young couple, extending her arms invitingly.

'Here we are. Please go in – and put the tea things on the little table over there in the corner. We'll have a grand time, the three of us! There's plenty of wine and sherry in the corner cupboard. Now, in you go.'

'Oh, Mrs Werle, it's awfully dark in here. Can you put on the light? We can't see a thing.'

'Just a second, dear. There's a switch in the corridor, here it is. Oh, my, the door's shutting! And it's so heavy,

impossible to open from this side . . . ! Well, well, well –
it can't be helped. You'll have to celebrate alone in there,
my dears. Take your time.'

And Agnete Werle bolted the heavy door with great care.

Standing for a moment outside, listening, she could
scarcely hear their shouts. Faint, oh so faint were the
voices heard here in the corridor. And nothing at all could
be heard from anywhere else in the house. Nothing at all.
This she knew for certain. Not even the screaming and
shouting of that traitor, the Norwegian Nazi, himself a
torturer, had been heard in that autumn of 1943. Served
him right, the rough treatment he'd got.

No room in the world could be more soundproof. And
no room could be more **hermetically** sealed – when the
valves in the ventilator were closed. They were now. They
could be regulated from the corridor.

'I hope they drink their tea first. It will put them to
sleep quite gently,' murmured the old lady on her way
upstairs. Ever so gently she chuckled as she sat down in
her favourite chair with *The Talented Mr Ripley*.

She looked forward to reading it, then to watching a
'Poirot' film on the telly at ten o'clock sharp.

'*Carpe diem*, that's a good maxim,' said Agnete
Werle, pleased.

'Excuse me, Inspector, I've got something very important
to tell you today.'

Chief Constable Ole Gregersen looked at the old lady
with a resigned expression. There was a troubled look in
her bright blue eyes. Her hat was askew on her snow-
white hair and her small thin fingers were clasping her
handbag. No way could he be angry with her, she was
such a sweet pathetic creature.

---

hermetically: tightly, absolutely (so that air cannot enter)
Carpe diem: 'seize the day' (Latin)

'What extraordinary things have happened now, Mrs Werle?' he asked patiently, far more patiently than he felt.

'I think something really peculiar and sinister has happened in my house, Mr Gregersen. There are actually *two* bodies, in my cellar. A young man and woman.'

'With knives in their backs, I presume?'

He winked mischievously and made a face at his assistant, Thea Dahl.

'No, no, Inspector, nothing of the sort! Would you imagine it, they're strangled, *choked*, both of them. Anyway, their faces are quite blue. Isn't it terrible? Do you think the murderer will be caught, Mr Gregersen?'

The policeman gave a sigh.

'You just go home to that nice house of yours and have another look and you'll find that everything's all right . . . But mind you, no more mystery books from now on. Why don't you read something nice, something edifying and uplifting for a change? Well, goodbye to you.'

The old lady walked slowly to the door, then abruptly turned round with a stern look at the policeman, cocking her head.

'What if I told you, Inspector, that I was the culprit – that it was I who killed the two poor creatures? Then you'd have to arrest me, wouldn't you, Mr Gregersen?'

'Shame on you, Mrs Werle! You are a wicked old lady, aren't you, in spite of being so sweet.' He took her gently by the arm and escorted her to the door.

'And now, Mrs Werle, please don't bother us again with that vivid imagination of yours.'

'All right, Inspector, I'll do as I'm told. But listen, shall I let the couple stay in the locked room in the cellar and never go into the room again as long as I live?'

'That's right, madam. Now off you go, have a nice walk home, and remember if someone is ever really unkind to you or tries to be violent – you know how young people can behave these days – you come straight here to us. It's lucky you don't live very far away.'

'Very well, Inspector. I'm glad to know there is some goodness in this cruel world. Goodbye, Mr Gregersen, and good day to you, Miss. And *thank you* with all my heart.'

The sweet old lady gave them a friendly nod and tripped out of the office.

Thea Dahl looked inquiringly at her superior.

'What on earth did she thank us like that for?'

'Hard to tell. She's very polite and well-bred, so why not? Well, she *is*, in spite of her crazy ideas.'

'Eccentric but harmless, isn't that how you put it, sir?'

'That's right, Miss Dahl. Eccentric but harmless.' The Chief Constable nodded, pleased with this apt description.

Woman and Home
Robert Westall

The house caught him, the first time he played truant from school.

Playing truant wasn't a habit. This was the first time. The trouble was, he was new at the school, and not fitting in. He'd come from a county grammar, and this was a city comprehensive. He had a posh accent he wasn't able to hide. Anyway, why should he? It was his voice.

He was bullied; but he didn't bully easy. He was tall and thin, but quick and not soft. When Brewster tried twisting his arm, he gave Brewster a very bloody nose. That should have finished it, especially as Brewster was far from heroic in defeat. It *would* have finished it, at his old grammar school.

But this was a city comprehensive, and not a well-run one. Brewster went to his Head of Year to complain, and it was the victim who got the telling-off.

'We don't hold with physical violence in this school,' said the Head. 'We find talking things out peacefully is better.'

He shook hands with Brewster in front of the Head. But afterwards Brewster was not inclined to talk things out peacefully; he summoned his gang. It never came to fists again. No, it was endless little things that weren't worth reporting. Like being tripped up in the corridor; or having your bag snatched from under your arm, and tipped out under the feet of the trampling herd. Or having 'London Pouf' scrawled on your locker-door with lipstick, or having your trousers dumped under the shower if you weren't back first from games.

They never seemed to tire of it. And after a month came the morning he just couldn't face any more of it. He turned away back towards the city centre.

He solved one problem, and immediately a lot of others landed on his head. Had any of his class seen him duck down the side-street? They would certainly report *him* to the form-master.

And here was one of them coming towards him up the side-street now . . .

He ducked away like a rabbit, into an even more ramshackle side-street, lined with rusty corrugated sheds in a sea of rose-bay willowherb, and realised the city centre wasn't for him today. It would be full of teachers nipping out to do a bit of shopping in their free period, governors who would recognise his uniform, his mum's new friends and neighbours . . .

So he wandered the back-streets; until it started to rain. Pretty heavily. Where on earth could he *go*? Mum only worked part time, and she would be home all day, doing the washing and ironing. They knew him at the library, the bowling-alley was shut; there was no cinema matineé till two o'clock, and *they'd* just ring school anyway.

The only place in the world was a derelict shed with the door hanging off its hinges. He slipped in like a thief. The floor was wet mud, a pattern of footprints filling with water from a big puddle in the middle. There were two big blue oil-drums lying on their sides, and a heap of black and white ash, where somebody had tried setting fire to the end wall. Somebody else had scrawled, in huge letters of yellow chalk, BANANA-LEGS IS A BUMMER.

Banana-legs was what they called the Head, because he braced his legs back tensely while waiting for something like silence to fall in assembly.

The evil-doers had been here before him; this was where *they* came when they were playing truant and it rained.

He was one of them now. He was sure some kid would have reported him. The Head would ring his mum. Trouble with Dad who was already worried sick about his new job . . .

He wished he was back in school. School might be hell, but it was better than *this*. He looked at his watch; an age seemed to have passed; but it was only twenty past nine. Soon they'd be coming out of assembly. If he ran, could he slip in with them to first lesson?

But he knew even if he ran like mad he'd never make it. He'd arrive wet and sweating in the middle of the lesson, to face questions and jeers.

The rain fell heavier, making a noise like machine-guns on the tin roof. What could he *do*?

First lesson was English. In a desperate attempt to be a law-abiding citizen, he got out his English book, sat on a blue oil-drum and tried to read. But it was too dark. And drops of water from the leaking roof began falling on his head.

The quality of the light changed. He looked up, to see a cat peering in the door. A cheerful-looking black cat, with a white bib. It seemed a godsend . . . he was good at making friends with cats. He held out his hand, called gently to it.

It gave him a look of sheer contempt and vanished.

Even the cat didn't want him . . .

He packed up his books in a frenzy; as he did so, his English exercise-book fell into the mud. Open. At the English essay he'd spent two hours on last night. A *good* essay, because he *liked* English.

He fastened his bag and ran out of that dreadful place like a mad thing; just wanting to get away. Anywhere.

That was when the house caught him.

It was the sun shining on the wet back of his neck that brought him to his senses. He looked around in surprise. It had stopped raining; the sky was blue, with only a few little friendly fluffy clouds. And he was utterly lost. But still he was afraid somebody might drive past in a car and see him. They said the Heads of Year spent half their days driving round the town looking for truants out of school. He *must* get under cover.

There was a high, overgrown privet hedge. A giant, obscene privet hedge like a young forest, ten feet high. And a double white gate. Half the gate was open. It drooped into the gravel as if it hadn't been moved in years. The paint was peeling off, leaving the wood beneath dark and soggy. Beyond, a worn gravel drive wound round to the left. There were tall thin fronds of grass growing out of the drive, all over. Dry and dead, last year's grass. Nobody must have gone up that drive for ages. It was *inviting*. Well, at least the passing cars wouldn't see him . . .

Even Brewster might've warned him. But Brewster wasn't there.

It was a funny garden. He helped Dad with the garden at home, so he soon spotted just how funny it was. Nobody had touched it for years; but it was OK. It hadn't turned into a jungle. He could see where weeds had tried to grow; but the weeds had died. They lay like shrivelled pale corpses though it was high summer. Whereas the garden plants and flowers were doing fine. Mind you, they needed pruning; the roses had put out branches ten feet high, that waved in the warm breeze like crazy fishing-rods. But they were doing OK.

Perhaps that should've warned him, too. But he passed up the formal garden, suddenly happy and peaceful and feeling at home. Up the stone steps, between the mossy pair of urns, up to the statue and the lily pond, where the white flowers were just breaking the surface, and the goldfish big as herring swam in the green depths. He wondered what the goldfish fed on . . .

He looked up, and saw the house.

He had to squint at it, because the sun was above it, and the sun was also reflecting up from the dark water of the lily pond.

He couldn't make out if anyone was at home or not. There was no smoke coming from the white chimneys, but then it was summer.

There were no broken windows, or slates off the roof. There were curtains at the windows, and stuff inside.

On the other hand, there was a white verandah with wistaria growing up the pillars. Lumps of the wistaria had grown out uncontrolled, and been tugged free of their wires by the wind, and hung in great loose clumps, swaying, as nobody who loved plants would've allowed. Nobody in their right mind would've allowed. They swayed crazily, dangerously.

The other odd thing was the half-bricks lying on the paths between him and the house. Not many, but placed temptingly. Tempting you to hurl them into the lily pond, or through the glass of the frail conservatory.

The temptation *annoyed* him; because he was not that sort of person. It wasn't that he was a goody-goody, or teacher's pet. It was because he *liked* lily ponds and conservatories and old houses . . . So he carefully picked the half-bricks from the paths, and tucked them away out of sight, before they tempted somebody else.

In the same way, when he reached the verandah, he couldn't help fastening back the wistaria inside its wires as best he could, and neatly pruning off the rest with his pocket-knife. It seemed to *want* to be done, somehow . . .

And then a door banged, round the corner of the verandah. He stood, paralysed with the knowledge that somebody lived here after all; blushing from head to foot with embarrassment that they must have been watching him, fiddling with their wistaria. Such enormous *cheek* . . . he waited, wild-eyed, trembling.

But the minutes passed, and nobody came. In the end, he moved, his legs stiff with tension. Round the corner . . .

There was a door. A double door, with glass panes in the top. One half was open. But as he watched, it swung closed in the wind, with the same bang. Then, in the next gust of wind, it swung open again.

And closed.

Then open again. The paint on the door was peeling off in great curls, like the paint on the gate. As the door slammed open and shut, great flakes fell off, to join flakes already lying on the verandah. It said quite clearly to him that nobody had lived there for ages. But if it was allowed to go on slamming in the wind, sooner or later the glass would break, the door would come off its hinges, the rain would get in.

He walked forward to shut the door safely.

And saw the huge heap of letters lying on the doormat inside. Like they'd found at home, when they came back from a fortnight's holiday. He peered down at them. The ones at the bottom were browning with age and rain and mingled with brown leaves that had blown in, but the ones on top looked quite new. Again, it offended him; it was a breach of the sensible world. He leaned through, and gathered them up, crouching on his heels and swaying dangerously, for he had a reluctance to put a foot inside. Then he retired to the fence of the verandah and sorted them into order by postmark. The oldest were over a year old, but some were only a week. Most of it was junk, addressed to 'The Occupier' but there was one addressed to 'Miss Nadine Marriner' in a small, mean, spidery hand. And somehow the name made him shudder, in spite of the warmth of the sun on his back. Miss Nadine Marriner – it had a thin spiteful sound, he thought.

There were a couple of elastic bands round some of the letters. He used them to make the whole thing into a neat bundle. But what to do with the bundle? He looked through the glass panes and saw a hall table, and a grandfather clock.

Well then, put them all on the hall table, slam the door shut properly, so it won't blow open again, and that was *that*. Somehow, although he liked the garden a lot, he didn't like the house so much. It looked dark inside, after the sunny garden.

He stepped in, and put the letters on the table. Looked at the grandfather clock. He sometimes went round the antique fairs with Dad. Dad liked to buy up old stopped clocks cheap, mend them, and sell them at a profit. Notes in your hand and not a word to the Inland Revenue.

This clock was stopped. But he could also see it was a very good one, with a silvered brass face, and brass tops to the columns, and a little brass eagle on top. Even with the dead leaves gathered in a drift round its base, it looked what Dad called a two-thousand-pound clock . . . He opened the door in the base, and looked inside. The pendulum was properly hung, the weights in place, but run down right to the floor. That was why the clock had stopped. He reached automatically for the shelf where keys were usually kept. The key was there. Unthinking, he put it into the winding-holes, and wound up the heavy weights and swung the pendulum.

Immediately the clock began to tick, a slow stately beat, that was a comfort to the ear. It seemed gently to bring the whole house alive.

Then suddenly, without warning, it chimed. Loud and long, it struck ten, though the hands pointed to half past two. He knew he shouldn't be alarmed. When clocks wound down, the chime sometimes got **out of synch**, as Dad said. But the chimes were so *loud* and triumphant; as if the clock was telling the whole house, the whole world, that he had come. He suddenly felt he had done something irrevocable. He turned to run . . .

He heard the door slam shut in the wind, behind him.

---

out of synch: not synchronised

Oh, well, open, shut, open, shut.

But when he pulled at the brass handle, green with lack of polishing, he found the lock had really worked this time. The door was really shut. And, what's more, struggle as he might, he couldn't get it open again.

Well, he told himself bravely, there will be other doors; or windows at a pinch, if they weren't painted up solid. He moved forward into the house, among the shadows. Outside, the sun had gone in . . .

He had a funny desire, every few paces, to stop and listen for other footsteps. Especially footsteps upstairs. That locked door made a difference. Before, one sound and he could have taken to his heels, and been out of the house and out of the garden in less than a minute. Now he was . . .

A prisoner. No longer free. If somebody came, he would have to do what they said . . .

The sooner he got out of here, the better.

He went into the first room with an open door. It seemed less cheeky. Less dangerous than trying one of the closed doors.

This was obviously the kitchen. Huge cold black kitchen range, and a battered electric cooker that must have been 1950s. Stone-flagged floor, with beetles scurrying away into the dark corners. The sink was full of dirty dishes, on to which the cold tap dripped, its sound quarrelling with the ticking of the clock that had followed him in. Every work-surface was covered with an intricate clutter, like a spider's web to catch the eye. He got a feel of Miss Nadine Marriner's mind, somehow. A muddled, devious, cluttered mind. He didn't like it. His mum kept their kitchen spotlessly tidy.

But the huge pine table in the middle of the kitchen held different kinds of things. A packet of cigarettes, with one taken out, smoked, and left as a trampled-out stub on the floor. A tin, with three crude rough-looking cigarettes inside, that smelt funny when he sniffed them. Reefers?

A bottle of whisky, half-empty. And a glass with a thin damp brown stain on the bottom.

He sniffed without touching. Yes, it was whisky all right.

Again, he was tempted. But he'd tried whisky, and hated the taste. And his first and only cigarette had made him sick. Besides, he didn't know where they'd been.

He left them alone.

He looked under the table. There was a huge dirty bundle there; a sleeping-bag wrapped round what looked like trousers and sweaters, with an enamel mug attached by a length of coarse white string.

A tramp's bundle. A man-tramp, from the smell of it.

So now he had a tramp to worry about as well. An old lady was one thing. But a tramp who probably stole whisky and reefers was a lot more scary.

C'mon, let's get out of here. Quick. He moved swiftly to the kitchen door. Undid the bolts, top and bottom. But it was locked as well, with a huge old-fashioned lock. And the key wasn't in it. He searched the cluttered work-surface in vain, feeling he was wasting time he could ill afford.

Well, other rooms then. With a verandah, there were bound to be french windows.

The next room did have french windows.

And a dog lying down next to them, asleep. Probably the tramp's dog. If he tried to get out through the french windows it might wake up and bark, or even attack him. The tramp would come. From upstairs. He kept having this funny feeling there was somebody upstairs.

He studied the dog carefully. It didn't look dangerous. It was a small brown mongrel, with floppy ears. Oh, he could deal with that. He tiptoed forwards, trying not to wake it. Reached the french windows, and twisted the handle.

It didn't open. He saw with despair the empty keyhole. Almost felt the dog reaching to bite his ankle. It must have heard, must have awakened.

But it still lay there. It lay there, still. *Too* still. Its belly wasn't going up and down. It wasn't *breathing*.

It must be *dead*. He looked down at it in horror. It still looked just . . . asleep. Comfortably asleep. There was no smell or maggots or any kind of nastiness, like fur falling off. Not like the dogs you saw floating drowned in the river . . .

He *had* to touch it. He didn't want to, but he *had* to.

It moved dryly, all of a piece, like a statue.

It was a stuffed dog. A real dog, real skin and fur, that had died and been stuffed. Nothing to do with any tramp. This had cost a lot of money. It must have been Miss Nadine Marriner's pet, that had died. She must have had it stuffed and gone on living with it.

What a crazy thing to do, living with a dead stuffed pet!

Then he wished he hadn't thought that. It wasn't nice to think Miss Nadine Marriner was crazy. But it explained the open door, and the leaves blowing in on priceless antiques, and the pile of unopened letters. He listened. Listened especially for ceilings creaking, which would mean somebody moving, upstairs. But there was just silence, and the ticking of the clock.

He looked longingly outside, through the glass of the french windows. There, at the end of the garden, was the drooping white gate. Beyond, cars would be passing. Far off, his class would be having their break. He could break the glass, get out that way. The sun was shining out there again.

But it wouldn't mean just breaking one pane of glass. It would mean breaking the french windows.

And he couldn't do that.

Well, there were plenty more rooms. Get on with it. You're just being silly. This is Monday morning the 3rd of

October 1988, and Mum is at home doing the washing. What could possibly happen?

As he turned to go back to the door, he saw the rocking chair. A big American rocker with a green upholstered back and seat. The upholstery was old, worn and greasy. And it seemed to bear the marks of a thin body, worn into it with time. There was a **hooky mat** beneath it, worn through to the canvas where two feet had pressed. There was a bag hanging on one arm of the chair, a cracked plastic bag, with a trail of tangled grey knitting dangling from it. On the other side of the chair, on the dusty carpet, was a cup and saucer, with a dry brown stain on the bottom.

He just knew this was where Miss Nadine Marriner had sat all day, knitting something the dullest grey colour imaginable. She was so much *there* that he gave a little humble apologetic bob of his head, and said absurdly, 'I'm sorry. I'm just going. When I can find a way out.'

The moment he spoke, he knew it was a mistake. Speaking to the chair made Miss Nadine Marriner more real in his mind. He could imagine her, now. Very thin, with gold-rimmed spectacles and grey hair pulled back in a bun, and knobbled veined thin hands, knitting, knitting. He couldn't *move*, for looking at the chair. He couldn't make his legs work, standing facing the empty chair, with the stuffed dog at his back.

Then with a yell like a feeble war-cry, he moved and leapt past the chair. As he passed it, he must have caught it with his sleeve. For when he glanced back from the doorway, it was rocking, rocking.

Frantic, now, he tried other doors. All were locked. And he could tell from trying to force the handles that they were very solid Victorian doors. And from under one came the foulest smell he had ever smelt. A smell of utter rottenness. Like the time they came back from holiday,

---

hooky mat: a rug made of looped wool on canvas

and the freezer had broken down, and the smell of that joint of pork Mum had been keeping for their return . . .

But he consoled himself that that door was plain, and next to the kitchen. Must be the pantry door. Some meat must have been left, and gone rotten inside. He thought he heard the buzz of a bluebottle, through the thick woodwork.

But he could've been imagining it. He knew he was in a very odd mood, one he'd never been in before. His body was shaky, his mind all whirly. He was starting to be silly and imagine things. He must get a grip on himself.

He must go upstairs. Look for keys, he told himself. So he wouldn't have to start smashing his way out . . . But he knew he was kidding himself.

Upstairs was calling him. He didn't want to go up there; he didn't want the shock of opening any more doors, of walking into rooms where he didn't know what he might see. The tramp asleep, snoring. Suddenly opening his eyes. Or Miss Nadine Marriner dead in her bed.

He hovered piteously in the hall, looking out through the glass in the door at the sunlit garden. Again, he contemplated smashing the glass, knocking out every sharp edge and crawling through to freedom. But suppose somebody came, while he was doing it . . .

Finally, he turned, and slowly began to climb the stairs. The stair-carpet was thick, but old and grey and full of dust. The dust shot up in clouds from his feet. Hung golden in the shafts of sunlight streaming down from the window on the landing above. The dust of Miss Nadine Marriner, creeping, sweet and sour, into his body through his nostrils, so he wanted to stop breathing.

And the sun was shining down the stairs so brightly, he couldn't see if there was anybody standing at the top of the stairs, waiting for him.

But there wasn't. There was just the window. It was clear in the middle (though very much spattered by dirty

rain) but blue and red stained-glass round the edges. Through it, he could see what appeared to be the kitchen garden. Again, not much in the way of weeds, but cabbages sprouting to a great height with yellow strings of flowers. And beyond the garden, quite far off, a kind of summer-house with glass windows.

And the window in the door was broken.

And through the jagged hole, he could see what looked like a flat bloated figure, half lying, half sitting inside. He might have thought it was a bundle of dark old clothes, except he could see the head, and a blurred sort of face, with dark holes for eyes, looking up at him in a rather pleading way. It gave him quite a turn, though it must have been fifty or sixty feet away, just sitting there, staring up at this window.

Then he realised it must be a made-up stuffed figure, a Guy Fawkes or a scarecrow, because the face was all weird colours, green and purple, and the eyes were just holes.

He had enough worries, without scarecrows stored in summer-houses. Find a key, and get out!

The first three doors were locked. Again he smelt, more faintly, the smell of rotting pork; but he thought it must be drifting upstairs from the larder. For it was *very* much fainter.

The last door was half open. But the room beyond was dim, as if the curtains were drawn. He hovered, listening. No sound at all; except the ticking of the clock, coming up the stairs behind. He sniffed. There was a very strong smell of old lady. Lavender and powder, old sweat and the sickly sweetness of age. He felt pulled forwards, as the receding waves had tried to suck him out to sea last summer. But he fought against it, now. As if he knew once he was sucked into that room, he would never come out again.

And then, downstairs, the clock struck eleven. The clang seemed to fill the whole house. And it was as if it was announcing his presence outside that door.

He was caught. He had to walk in.

There was a figure standing straight opposite him, in the gloom of the drawn curtains. A figure that watched him with eyes that glared out of a white face, standing stock-still.

It was no bigger than he himself. It made no move to attack, standing with its arms by its sides. It looked . . .

Hopeless, helpless, drowned in the green gloom.

He half raised an arm, to ward off the terrified glare.

The figure in turn raised its arm.

And then he saw it was himself; caught in the long mirror of a wardrobe. But lost, drowned, frozen as if under green ice.

He tried to force a laugh; it failed, making a weird mad sound in that dim silent room. But it released him to move.

He swung round to look behind the door, where the bed would be . . .

The bed was made, pulled flat and tight. Nothing to be afraid of there. He looked under the bed; nothing but the dim shine of a white chamber pot. He let his eyes pan to the left. A chair with a heap of old lady's dark clothes piled up on it. Another mirror, above a dressing-table, as cluttered as the kitchen work-surfaces downstairs. Miss Nadine Marriner's, without a doubt. Then a tall dark chest of drawers, with half the drawers pulled open, and pale female things hanging out.

Then the big white marble fireplace, and above it . . .

Miss Nadine Marriner stared down at him.

Larger than life. Seated in the rocking-chair from downstairs, with her knobbled veined hands clutching the wooden arms with a grip that said 'Mine, mine, *mine*!' she looked exactly as he had imagined her, when he first saw the rocking-chair. Tall, very bony, with gold-rimmed spectacles and her grey hair pulled back tight in a bun.

A portrait. A picture in oils, in a huge gilt frame. Just a huge oil-painting. But how could he have known so exactly what she would look like, before he saw the portrait?

And why did the face stare at him so, the eyes seeming to burn right through him, as if she was alive? Why did it make him feel so small, so helpless, so . . . obedient? Why did her presence seem to fill the whole room, the whole house? And why did he stand so submissive, waiting for her to . . .

Speak. He was waiting for her to speak; to give him orders. To obey her every whim, even as he saw, without hope, the cruelty in her, the lack of any sort of kindness or mercy.

He waited.

And then he saw the picture was a little crooked; it sloped down a little to the right.

He must set it straight. Slowly he walked up to it, closer and closer to those claw hands, those piercing eyes.

He tried to straighten the picture by grasping the two bottom corners. But the picture wouldn't move; it seemed stuck to the wall. He tried to pull it away, towards him.

As it moved and straightened, something fell down from behind it, bounced on the marble top of the mantelpiece, and fell among the soot-splashes that the rain had left on the green tiles of the hearth.

A thick brown letter.

Well, he couldn't just leave it there, getting dirty among the soot. He picked it up, and read the writing on the envelope.

TO THE FINDER.

That was *him*. And he was in no state to disobey the tall, spiky, spidery handwriting of Miss Nadine Marriner.

Inside was another envelope, and a note.

The note said, DELIVER THIS BY HAND TO THE ADDRESS ON THE ENVELOPE.

The envelope was addressed to a firm of solicitors in the city centre. It was open, and he could not help being curious. He looked up at the piercing eyes of Miss Nadine Marriner, and strangely they did not forbid him.

He opened the envelope, and unfolded the large stiff piece of paper. It was headed, THE LAST WILL AND TESTAMENT OF NADINE MARRINER, DECEASED.

He shuddered a little, and read on.

> I AM DEAD. HAVE NO DOUBT ABOUT THAT. DO NOT LOOK FOR MY CORPSE. YOU WILL NEVER FIND IT. I AM IN A VERY SAFE PLACE.
>
> BUT I LEAVE MY HOUSE, LANDS, AND ALL I AM POSSESSED OF TO THE BEARER OF THIS LETTER. I HAVE FOUND HIM HONEST AND TRUSTWORTHY. HE WILL CARE FOR THE HOUSE AND MY POSSESSIONS NOW I AM DEAD. HE GETS IT ONLY ON CONDITION THAT HE SELLS NOTHING, BUT LIVES IN THIS HOUSE, AND KEEPS IT AS IT IS AND IN GOOD REPAIR AS LONG AS HE SHALL LIVE.
>
> AND FOR THE OTHERS WHO CAME, THE THIEVES WHO TRIED TO STEAL, THE VANDALS WHO CAME TO SMASH AND BURN, FIND THEM WHERE YOU MAY AND BURY THEM WHERE YOU WILL. THEY BROUGHT THEIR DEATH UPON THEMSELVES.

There was more, and signatures at the bottom. Miss Nadine Marriner and two others he couldn't read.

The phrases hammered through his head. 'They brought their death upon themselves . . . Find them where you may and bury them where you will.'

He remembered the bloated green-faced scarecrow who had glared up at him so pleadingly from the broken glass of the summer-house. The awful smell in the room downstairs . . . The whole house was a *trap*. He remembered the half-bricks he had been tempted to throw in the lily pond, and at the frail conservatory. The whisky and the cigarettes and the reefers on the kitchen table. How many more traps?

And he knew she *was* still here. In the house. He had a weird feeling she was behind that tomb-like marble fireplace, still sitting upright in her chair, her hands clutched on the arms, saying 'Mine, mine, *mine*.' The whole house was full of her. It was as if she had moved out of her tall frail body, into the bricks and mortar, the glass and wood, the very soil itself, poisoning the intruding weeds . . . What had the huge goldfish fed on, to stay alive all this time?

There was no way out. He was trapped, finished. He must obey her, or he would never get out of here. And if he obeyed her, he would be caught up with her in a bargain, till the day he died . . .

And then he remembered the pile of letters on the doormat. The postman must have walked up the path nearly every day, and walked out again untouched.

Because he was innocent. Because he was just delivering letters, whistling to himself, thinking about something else.

It gave him a bit of courage. Enough to put everything back in the big envelope, and to say firmly, 'No thanks,' and to lift the portrait and tuck the letter back where it had come from.

He was frightened it might fall out again; with a dreadful insistence; as a dreadful warning.

But it stayed where it was. So he went while the going was good. Down the dust-laden stairs, to the front door. Through its glass he could see his schoolbag lying on the verandah, where he'd left it, what seemed like half a lifetime ago.

He put his hand on the dark-green brass of the door handle and tried it.

It turned first time, and he grabbed his bag and was off the verandah, tearing past the goldfish pond, down the steps between the urns, and out through the white gate.

He was still running when he heard a voice bellow.

'*HIGGINSON!*'

He stopped because that was his name. He had a feeling that the voice had been bellowing it for some time.

He was in the city centre, between the McDonald's and the video shop. He had no idea what streets he had run down. What streets he must have crossed, though he had a vague memory of car-horns hooting.

'Higginson? Where the hell do you think you are going? What's got into you, lad?'

It was Toddser Todd, Head of Third Year, glaring at him through the wound-down window of his Ford Fiesta, his red face clashing horribly with his ginger hair.

He didn't like Toddser much; didn't trust him. But at that moment, he felt like flinging his arms around his neck. But he only went over, and leaned against the car's bonnet, shaking all over.

'Get in,' said Toddser. 'You're in trouble, real trouble. This will have to go to the Head. You kids think you can get away with murder . . .'

He got in, and held his bag tight on his knee, so that Toddser wouldn't see how much his legs were shaking. But Toddser wasn't interested. He was still cruising the town centre, peering down every street they came to, looking for other truants, and at the same time mumbling the same old crap about order and discipline that he must mumble to all the kids he caught. But you could tell he was pleased to have caught somebody; you could tell he enjoyed the game.

'You're in *real* trouble,' went on Toddser like a tape-recording. 'You don't know what real trouble is like, till now . . .'

'I won't do it again, sir,' he said, with a great deal of fervour. So that Toddser, halted at a traffic-light, stared at him as if he was seeing him for the first time and said,

'You sound as if you really mean it.'

Then the lights changed, and Toddser drove back to school, and he closed his eyes and relaxed into the paradise of the real trouble to come. Knowing he could never find that white gate again. Even if he *tried*.

Farthing House
Susan Hill

I have never told you any of this before – I have never told
anyone, and indeed, writing it down and sealing it up in
an envelope to be read at some future date may still not
count as 'telling'. But I shall feel better for it, I am sure of
that. Now it has all come back to me, I do not want to let
it go again, I must set it down.

It is true, and for that very reason you must not hear it
just now. You will be prey to enough anxieties and fancies
without my adding ghosts to them; the time before the
birth of a child one is so very vulnerable.

I daresay that it has made me vulnerable too, that this
has brought the events to mind.

I began to be restless several weeks ago. I was burning
the last of the leaves. It was a most beautiful day, clear and
cold and blue and a few of them were swirling down as
I raked and piled. And then a light wind blew suddenly
across the grass, scuttling the leaves and making the
woodsmoke drift towards me, and as I caught the smell of
it, that most poignant, melancholy, nostalgic of all smells,
something that had been drifting on the edges of my
consciousness blurred and insubstantial, came into focus,
and in a rush I remembered . . .

It was as though a door had been opened on to the
past, and I had stepped through and gazed at what I saw
there again. I saw the house, the drive sweeping up to it,
the countryside around it, on that late November
afternoon, saw the red sun setting behind the beech
copse, beyond the rising, brown fields, saw the bonfire
the gardener had left to smoulder on gently by itself, and
the thin pale smoke coiling up from its heart. I was there,
all over again.

I went in a daze into the house, made some tea, and sat, still in my old, outdoor clothes at the kitchen table, as it went quite dark outside the window, and I let myself go back to that day, and the nights that followed, watched it all unfold again, remembered. So that it was all absolutely clear in my mind when the newspaper report appeared, a week later.

I was going to see Aunt Addy. It was November, and she had been at the place called Farthing House since the New Year, but it was only now that I had managed to get away and make the two hundred-mile journey to visit her.

We had written, of course, and spoken on the telephone, and so far as I could tell she sounded happy. Yes, they were very nice people, she said, and yes, it was such a lovely house, and she did so like her room, everyone was most kind, oh yes dear, it was the right thing, I should have done it long ago, I really am very settled.

And Rosamund said that she was, too, said that it was fine, really, just as Addy told me, a lovely place, such kind people, and Alec had been and he agreed.

All the same, I was worried, I wasn't sure. She had been so independent always, so energetic, so very much her own person all her life, I couldn't see her in a Home, however nice and however sensible a move it was – and she was eighty-six and had had two nasty falls the previous winter – I liked to think of her as she was when we were children, and went to stay at the house in Wales, striding over the hills with the dogs, rowing on the lake, getting up those colossal picnics for us all. I always loved her, she was such fun. I wish you had known her.

And of course, I wish that one of us could have had her, but there really wasn't room to make her comfortable and, oh, other feeble-sounding reasons, which are real reasons, nonetheless.

She had never asked me to visit her, that wasn't her way. Only the more she didn't ask, the more I knew that I should, the guiltier I felt. It was just such a terrible year, what with one thing and another.

But now I was going. It had been a beautiful day for the drive too. I had stopped twice, once in a village, once in a small market town and explored churches and little shops, and eaten lunch and had a pot of tea and taken a walk along the banks of a river in the late sunshine, and the berries, I remember, had been thick and heavy, clustered on the boughs. I'd seen a jay and two deer and once, like magic, a kingfisher, flashing blue as blue across a hump-backed bridge. I'd had a sort of holiday really. But now I was tired, I would be glad to get there. It was very nice that they had a guest-room, and I didn't have to stay alone in some hotel. It meant I could really spend all my time with Aunt Addy. Besides, you know how I've always hated hotels, I lie awake thinking of the hundreds of people who've slept in the bed before me.

Little Dornford 1½m.

But as I turned right and the road narrowed to a single track, between trees, I began to feel nervous, anxious, I prayed that it really would be all right, that Aunt Addy had been telling the truth.

'You'll come to the church', they had said, and a row of three cottages, and then there is the sign to Farthing House, at the bottom of the drive.

I had seen no other car since leaving the cathedral town seven miles back on the main road. It was very quiet, very out of the way. I wondered if Addy minded. She had always been alone up there in her own house but somehow now that she was so old and infirm, I thought she might have liked to be nearer some bustle, perhaps actually in a town. And what about the others, a lot of old women isolated out here together? I shivered suddenly and peered forwards along the darkening lane. The church was just ahead, the car lights swept along a yew hedge, a **lych gate**, caught the shoulder of a gravestone. I slowed down.

FARTHING HOUSE. It was a neat, elegantly lettered sign, not too prominent and at least it did not proclaim itself Residential Home.

The last night was fading in the sky behind a copse of bare beech trees, the sun dropping down, a great red, frost-rimmed ball. I saw the drive, a wide lawn, the remains of a bonfire of leaves, smouldering by itself in a corner. Farthing House.

I don't know exactly what my emotions had been up to that moment. I was very tired, with that slightly dazed, confused sensation that comes after a long drive and the attendant concentration. And I was apprehensive. I so wanted to be happy about Aunt Addy, to be sure that she was in the right place to spend the rest of her life – or maybe I just wanted to have my conscience cleared so I could bowl off home again in a couple of days with a blithe heart, untroubled by guilt and be able to enjoy the coming Christmas.

But as I stood on the black and white marbled floor of the entrance porch I felt something else and it made me hesitate before ringing the bell. What was it? Not fear or anxiety, no shudders. I am being very careful now, it would be too easy to claim that I had sensed something sinister, that I was shrouded at once in the atmosphere of a haunted house.

But I did not, nothing of that sort crossed my mind. I was only overshadowed by a curious sadness – I don't know exactly how to describe it – a sense of loss, a melancholy. It descended like a damp veil about my head and shoulders. But it lifted, or almost, the cloud passed after a few moments. Well, I was tired, I was cold, it was

---

lych gate: gate at the entrance to a churchyard

the back end of the year, and perhaps I had caught a   ,
which often manifests itself first as a sudden change of
mood into a lower key.

The only other thing I noticed was the faintest smell of
hospital antiseptic. That depressed me a bit more.
Farthing House wasn't a hospital or even a nursing home
proper and I didn't want it to seem so to Aunt Addy, not
even in this slight respect.

But in fact, once I was inside, I no longer noticed it at
all, there was only the pleasant smell of furniture polish,
and fresh chrysanthemums and, somewhere in the
background, a light, spicy smell of baking.

The smells that greeted me were all of a piece with the
rest of the welcome. Farthing House seemed like an
individual, private home. The antiques in the hall were
good, substantial pieces and they had been well cared for
over the years, there were framed photographs on a
sideboard, flowers in jugs and bowls, there was an old,
fraying, tapestry-covered armchair on which a fat cat slept
beside a fire. It was quiet, too, there was no rattling of
trolleys or buzzing of bells. And the matron did not call
herself one.

'You are Mrs Flower – how nice to meet you.' She put
out her hand. 'Janet Pearson.'

She was younger than I had expected, probably in her
late forties. A small King Charles spaniel hovered about
her waving a frond-like tail. I relaxed.

I spent a good evening in Aunt Addy's company; she
was so settled and serene, and yet still so full of life.
Farthing House was well run, warm and comfortable, and
there was good, home-cooked dinner with fresh
vegetables and an excellent lemon meringue pie. The
rooms were spacious, the other residents pleasant but
not over-obtrusive.

Something else was not as I had expected. It had been
necessary to reserve the guest-room and bathroom well

in advance, but when Mrs Pearson herself took my bag
and led me up the handsome staircase, she told me that
after a serious leak in the roof had caused damage, it was
being redecorated. 'So I've put you in Cedar – it happens
to be free just now.' She barely hesitated as she spoke,
'And it's such a lovely room, I'm sure you'll like it.'

How could I have failed? Cedar Room was one of the
two largest in the house, on the first floor, with big bay
windows overlooking the garden at the back – though
now the deep red curtains had been drawn against the
early evening darkness.

'Your aunt is just across the landing.'

'So they've put you in Cedar,' Addy said later when we
were having a drink in her own room. It wasn't so large
but I preferred it simply, I think, because there was so
much familiar furniture, her chair, her own oak dresser,
the painted screen, even the club fender we used to sit on
to toast our toes as children.

'Yes. It seems a bit big for one person, but it's very
handsome. I'm surprised it's vacant.'

Addy winked at me. 'Well, of course it *wasn't* . . .'

'Oh.' For an instant, that feeling of unease and
melancholy passed over me like a shadow again.

'Now buck up, don't look wan, there isn't time.' And
she plunged me back into family chat and cheerful
recollections, interspersed with sharp observations about
her fellow residents, so that I was almost entirely
comfortable again.

I remained so until we parted at getting on for half past
eleven. We had spent much of the evening alone
together, and then joined some of the others in one of
the lounges, where an almost party-like atmosphere had
developed, with laughter and banter and happy talk,
which had all helped to revive my first impressions of
Farthing House and Addy's place there.

It was not until I closed the door of my room and was alone that I was forced to acknowledge again what had been at the back of my mind all the time, almost like having a person at my shoulder, though just out of sight. I was in this large, high-ceilinged room because it was free, its previous occupant having recently died. I knew no more, and did not want to know, had firmly refrained from asking any questions. Why should it matter? It did not. As a matter of fact it still does not, it had no bearing at all on what happened, but I must set it down because I feel I have to tell the whole truth and part of that truth is that I was in an unsettled, slightly nervous frame of mind as I got ready for bed, because of what I knew, and because I could not help wondering whether whoever had occupied Cedar Room had died in it, perhaps even in this bed. I was, as you might say, almost expecting to have bad dreams or to see a ghost.

There is just one other thing.

When we were all in the lounge, the talk had inevitably been of former homes and families, the past in general, and Addy had wanted some photographs from upstairs. I had slipped out to fetch them for her.

It was very quiet in the hall. The doors were heavy and soundproof, though from behind one I could just hear some faint notes of recorded music, but the staff quarters down the passage were closed off and silent.

So I was quite certain that I heard it, the sound was unmistakable. It was a baby crying. Not a cat, not a dog. They are quite different, you know. What I heard from some distant room on the ground floor was the cry of a newborn baby.

I hesitated. Stopped. But it was over at once, and it did not come again. I waited, feeling uncertain. But then, from the room with the music, I heard the muffled signature tune of the ten o'clock news. I went on up the staircase. The noise had come from the television then.

Except, you see, that deep down and quite surely, I knew that it had not.

I may have had odd **frissons** about my room but once I was actually in bed and settling down to read a few pages of *Sense and Sensibility* before going to sleep, I felt quite composed and cheerful. The only thing wrong was that the room still seemed far too big for one person. There was ample furniture and yet it was as though someone else ought to be there. I find it difficult to explain precisely.

I was very tired. And Addy was happy, Farthing House was everything I had hoped it would be, I had had a most enjoyable evening, and the next day we were to go out and see something of the countryside and later, hear sung evensong at the cathedral.

I switched out the lamp.

At first I thought it was as quiet outside the house as in, but after a few minutes, I heard the wind sifting through the bare branches and sighing towards the windows and away. I felt like a child again, snug in my little room under the eaves.

I slept.

I dreamed almost at once with extraordinary vividness, and it was, at least to begin with, a most happy dream. I was in St Mary's, the night after you were born, lying in my bed in that blissful, glowing, untouchable state when the whole of the rest of life seems suspended and everything irrelevant but this. You were there in your crib beside me, though I did not look at you. I don't think anything happened in the dream and it did not last very long. I was simply there in the past and utterly content.

I woke with a start, and as I came to, it was with that sound in my ears, the crying of the baby that I had heard as I crossed the hall earlier that evening. The room was

---

frissons: shivers

quite dark. I knew at once where I was and yet I was still half within my dream – I remember that I felt a spurt of disappointment that it had *been* a dream and I was actually there, a new young mother again with you beside me in the crib.

How strange, I thought, I wonder why. And then something else happened – or no, not 'happened'. There just *was* something else, that is the only way I can describe it.

I had the absolutely clear sense that someone else had been in my room – not the hospital room of my dream, but this room in Farthing House. No one was here now, but minutes before I woke, I knew that they had been. I remember thinking, someone is in the next bed. But of course, there was no next bed, just mine.

After a while I switched on the lamp. All was as it had been when I had gone to sleep. Only that sensation, that atmosphere was still there. If nothing else had happened at Farthing House, I suppose in time I would have decided I had half-dreamed, half-imagined it, and forgotten. It was only because of what happened afterwards that I remembered so clearly and knew with such certainty that my feeling had been correct.

I got up, went over to the tall windows and opened the curtains a little. There was a clear, star-pricked sky and a thin paring of moon. The gardens and the dark countryside all around were peaceful and still.

But I felt oppressed again by the most profound melancholy of spirit, the same terrible sadness and sense of loss that had overcome me on my arrival. I stood there for a long time, unable to release myself from it, before going back to bed to read another chapter of Jane Austen, but I could not concentrate properly and in the end grew drowsy. I heard nothing, saw nothing, and I did not dream again.

The next morning my mood had lightened. There had been a slight frost during the night, and the sun rose on a countryside dusted over with **rime**. The sky was blue, trees set in dark pencil strokes against it.

We had a good day, Aunt Addy and I, enjoying one another's company, exploring churches and antique shops, having a pub lunch, and an old-fashioned muffin and fruitcake tea after the cathedral service.

It was as we were eating it that I asked suddenly, 'What do you know about Farthing House?'

Seeing Addy's puzzled look, I went on, 'I just mean, how long has Mrs Pearson been there, who had it before, all that sort of thing. Presumably it was once a family house.'

'I have an idea someone told me it had been a military convalescent home during the war. Why do you ask?'

I thought of Cedar Room the previous night, and that strange sensation. *What* had it been? Or who? But I found that I couldn't talk about it for some reason, it made me too uneasy. 'Oh, nothing. Just curious.' I avoided Addy's eye.

That evening, the matron invited me to her own room for sherry, and to ask if I was happy about my aunt. I reassured her, saying all the right, polite things. Then she said, 'And have you been quite comfortable?'

'Oh yes.' I looked straight at her. I thought she might have been giving me an opening – I wasn't sure. And I almost did tell her. But again, I couldn't speak of it. Besides, what was there to tell? I had heard a baby crying – from the television. I'd had an unusual dream, and an odd, confused sensation when I woke from it that someone had just left my room.

Nothing.

'I've been extremely comfortable,' I said firmly. 'I feel quite happy about everything.'

---

rime: white frost

Did she relax just visibly, smile a little too eagerly, was there a touch of relief in her voice when she next spoke?

I don't know whether or not I dreamed that night. It seemed that one minute I was in a deep sleep, and the next that something had woken me. As I came to, I know I heard the echo of crying in my ears, or in my inner ear, but a different sort of crying this time, not that of a baby, but a desperate, woman's sobbing. The antiseptic smell was faintly there again too, my awareness of it was mingled with that of the sounds.

I sat bolt upright. The previous night, I had had the sensation of someone having just been in my room.

Now, I saw her.

There was another bed in the opposite corner of the room, close to the window, and she was getting out of it. The room felt horribly cold. I remember being conscious of the iciness on my hands and face.

I was wide awake, I am quite sure of that, I could hear my own heart pounding, see the bedside table, and the lamp and the blue binding of *Sense and Sensibility* in the moonlight. I know I was not dreaming, so much so that I almost spoke to the woman, wondering as I saw her what on earth they were thinking of to put her and her bed in my room while I was asleep.

She was young, with a flowing, embroidered nightgown, high necked and long sleeved. Her hair was long too, and as pale as her face. Her feet were bare. But I could not speak to her, my throat felt paralysed. I tried to swallow, but even that was difficult, the inside of my mouth was so dry.

She seemed to be crying. I suppose that was what I had heard. She moved across the room towards the door and she held out her arms as if she were begging someone to give her something. And that terrible melancholy came over me again, I felt inconsolably hopeless and sad.

The door opened. I know that because a rush of air came in to the room, and it went even colder, but somehow, I did not see her put her hand to the knob and turn it. All I know is that she had gone, and that I was desperate to follow her, because I felt that she needed me in some way.

I did not switch on the lamp or put on my dressing gown, I half-ran to catch her up.

The landing outside was lit as if by a low, flickering candle flame. I saw the door of Aunt Addy's room but the wood looked darker, and there were some pictures on the walls that I had not noticed before. It was still so cold my breath made little haws of white in front of my face.

The young woman had gone. I went to the head of the staircase. Below, it was pitch dark. I heard nothing, no footstep, no creak of the floorboards. I was too frightened to go any further.

As I turned, I saw that the flickering light had faded and the landing was in darkness too. I felt my way, trembling, back to my own room and put my hand on the doorknob. As I did so I heard from far below, in the recesses of the house, the woman's sobbing and a calling – it might have been of a name, but it was too faint and far away for me to make it out.

I managed to stumble across the room and switch on the lamp. All was normal. There was just one bed, my own. Nothing had changed.

I looked at the clock. It was a little after three. I was soaked in sweat, shaking, terrified. I did not sleep again that night but sat up in the chair wrapped in the eiderdown with the lamp on, until the late grey dawn came around the curtains. That I had seen a young woman, that she had been getting out of another bed in my room, I had no doubt at all. I had not been dreaming, as I certainly had on the previous night. The difference between the two experiences was quite clear to me. She had been there.

I had never either believed or disbelieved in ghosts, scarcely ever thought about the subject at all. Now, I knew that I had seen one. And I could not throw off not only my fear but the depression her presence inflicted on me. Her distress and agitation, whatever their cause, had affected me profoundly, and from the first moment of my arrival at the door of Farthing House. It was a dark, dreadful, helpless feeling and with it there also went a sense of foreboding.

I was due to leave for home the following morning but when I joined Aunt Addy for breakfast I felt wretched, tense and strained, quite unfit for a long drive. When I went to Mrs Pearson's office and explained simply that I had not slept well, she expressed concern at once and insisted that I stay on another night. I wanted to, but I did not want to remain in Cedar Room. When I mentioned it, very diffidently, Mrs Pearson gave me a close look and I waited for her to question me but she did not, only told me, slipping her pen nervously round and round between her fingers, that there simply was not another vacant room in the house. So I said that of course it did not matter, it was only that I had always felt uneasy sleeping in very large rooms, and laughed it off, trying to reassure her. She pretended that I had.

That morning, Aunt Addy had an appointment with the visiting hairdresser. I didn't feel like sitting about reading papers and chatting in the lounge. They were nice women, the other residents, kind and friendly and welcoming but I was on edge and still enveloped in sadness and foreboding. I needed time to myself.

The weather didn't help. It had gone a degree or two warmer and the rise in temperature had brought a dripping fog and low cloud that masked the lines of the countryside. I trudged around Farthing House gardens but the grass was soaking wet and the sight of the dreary bushes and black trees lowered my spirits further. I set off down the lane, past the three cottages. A dog barked from one, but the others were silent and apparently empty. I suppose that by then I had begun to wallow slightly in my mood and I decided that I might as well go the whole hog and visit the church and its overgrown little graveyard. It was bitterly cold inside. There were some good brasses and a wonderful ornate eighteenth-century monument to a pious local squire, with florid rhymes and madly grieving angels. But the stained glass was ugly in '**uncut moquette**' colours, as Stephen would have said, and besides it was actually colder inside the church than out.

I had a prowl around the graveyard, looking here and there at epitaphs. There were a couple of minor gems but otherwise, all was plain, names and dates and dullness and I was about to leave when my eye was caught by some gravestones at the far side near to the field wall. They were set a little apart and neatly arranged in two rows. I bent down and deciphered the faded inscriptions. They were all the graves of babies, newborn or a few days old, and dating from the early years of the century. I wondered why so many, and why all young babies. They had different surnames, though one or two recurred. Had there been some dreadful epidemic in the village? Had the village been much larger then, if there had been so many young families?

At the far end of the row were three adult sized stones. The inscriptions of two had been mossed over but one was clear.

Eliza Maria Dolly.
Died January 20 1902. Aged 19 years.
And also her infant daughter.

---

uncut moquette: type of furnishing fabric

As I walked thoughtfully back I saw an elderly man dismount from a bicycle beside the gate and pause, looking towards me.

'Good morning! Gerald Manberry, vicar of the parish. Though really I am semi-retired, there isn't a great deal for a full-time man to take care of nowadays. I see you have been looking at the poor little Farthing House graves.'

'Farthing House?'

'Yes, just down the lane. It was a home for young women and their illegitimate babies from the turn of the century until the last war. Then a military convalescent home, I believe. It's a home for the elderly now, of course.'

How bleak that sounded. I told him that I had been staying there. 'But the graves . . .' I said.

'I suppose a greater number of babies died around the time of birth then, especially in those circumstances. And mothers too, I fear. Poor girls. It's all much safer now. A better world. A better world.'

I watched him wheel his ancient bicycle round to the vestry door, before beginning to walk back down the empty lane towards Farthing House. But I was not seeing my surroundings or hearing the caw-cawing of the rooks in the trees above my head. I was seeing the young woman in the nightgown, her arms outstretched, and hearing her cry and feeling again that terrible sadness and distress. I thought of the grave of Eliza Maria Dolly, 'and also her infant daughter'.

I was not afraid any more, not now that I knew who she was and why she had been there, getting out of her bed in Cedar Room, to go in search of her baby. Poor, pale, distraught young thing, she could do no one harm.

I slept well that night, I saw nothing, heard nothing, although in the morning I knew, somehow, that she had been there again, there was the same emptiness in the room and the imprint of her sad spirit upon it.

The fog had cleared and it was a pleasant winter day, intermittently sunny. I left for home after breakfast, having arranged that Aunt Addy was to come to us for Christmas.

She did so and we had a fine time, as happy as we all used to be together, with Stephen and I, Rosamund, Alec and the others. I shall always be glad of that, for it was Addy's last Christmas. She fell down the stairs at Farthing House the following March, broke her hip and died of a stroke a few days later. They took her to hospital and I saw her there, but afterwards, when her things were to be cleared up, I couldn't face it. Stephen and Alec did everything. I never went back to Farthing House.

I often thought about it though, even dreamed of it. An experience like that affects you profoundly and for ever. But I could not have spoken about it, not to anyone at all. If ever a conversation touched upon the subject of ghosts I kept silent. I had seen one. I knew. That was all.

Some years afterwards, I learned that Farthing House had closed to residents, been sold and then demolished, to make room for a new development – the nearby town was spreading out now. Little Dornford had become a suburb.

I was sad. It had been, in most respects, such a good and happy place.

Then, only a week ago, I saw the name again, quite by chance, it leapt at me from the newspaper. You may remember the case, though you would not have known of any personal connection.

A young woman stole a baby, from its pram outside a shop. The child had only been left for a moment or two but apparently she had been following and keeping watch, waiting to take it. It was found eventually, safe and well. She had looked after it, so I suppose things could have been worse, but the distress caused to the parents was obviously appalling. You can imagine that now, can't you?

They didn't send her to prison, she was taken into medical care. Her defence was that she had stolen the child when she was out of her right mind after the death of her own baby not long before. The child was two days old. Her address was given as Farthing House Close, Little Dornford.

I think of it constantly, see the young, pale, distraught woman, her arms outstretched, searching, hear her sobbing, and the crying of her baby.

But I imagine that she has gone, now that she has what she was looking for.

My Oedipus Complex*
Frank O'Connor

Father was in the army all through the war – the First War, I mean – so, up to the age of five, I never saw much of him, and what I saw did not worry me. Sometimes I woke and there was a big figure in khaki peering down at me in the candlelight. Sometimes in the early morning I heard the slamming of the front door and the clatter of nailed boots down the cobbles of the lane. These were Father's entrances and exits. Like Santa Claus he came and went mysteriously.

In fact, I rather liked his visits, though it was an uncomfortable squeeze between Mother and him when I got into the big bed in the early morning. He smoked, which gave him a pleasant musty smell, and shaved, an operation of astounding interest. Each time he left a trail of souvenirs – model tanks and Gurkha knives with handles made of bullet cases, and German helmets and cap badges and button-sticks, and all sorts of military equipment – carefully stowed away in a long box on top of the wardrobe, in case they ever came in handy. There was a bit of the magpie about Father; he expected everything to come in handy. When his back was turned, Mother let me get a chair and rummage through his treasures. She didn't seem to think so highly of them as he did.

The war was the most peaceful period of my life. The window of my attic faced south-east. My Mother had curtained it, but that had small effect. I always woke with the first light and, with all the responsibilities of the previous day melted, feeling myself rather like the sun,

---

*In Greek mythology, King Oedipus was in love with his mother

ready to illumine and rejoice. Life never seemed so
simple and clear and full of possibilities as then. I put my
feet out from under the clothes – I called them Mrs Left
and Mrs Right – and invented dramatic situations for
them in which they discussed the problems of the day. At
least Mrs Right did; she was very demonstrative, but
I hadn't the same control of Mrs Left, so she mostly
contented herself with nodding agreement.

They discussed what Mother and I should do during
the day, what Santa Claus should give a fellow for
Christmas, and what steps should be taken to brighten
the home. There was that little matter of the baby, for
instance. Mother and I could never agree about that. Ours
was the only house in the terrace without a new baby, and
Mother said we couldn't afford one until Father came
back from the war because they cost seventeen and six.
That showed how simple she was. The Geneys up the
road had a baby, and everyone knew they couldn't afford
seventeen and six. It was probably a cheap baby, and
Mother wanted something really good, but I felt she was
too exclusive. The Geneys' baby would have done us fine.

Having settled my plans for the day, I got up, put a chair
under the attic window, and lifted the frame high enough
to stick out my head. The window overlooked the front
gardens of the terrace behind ours, and beyond these it
looked over a deep valley to the tall, red-brick houses
terraced up the opposite hillside, which were all still in
shadow, while those at our side of the valley were all lit
up, though with long strange shadows that made them
seem unfamiliar; rigid and painted.

After that I went into Mother's room and climbed into
the big bed. She woke and I began to tell her of my
schemes. By this time, though I never seem to have
noticed it, I was **petrified** in my nightshirt, and I thawed

---

petrified: turned into stone

as I talked until, the last frost melted, I fell asleep beside her and woke again only when I heard her below in the kitchen, making the breakfast.

After breakfast we went into town; heard Mass at St Augustine's and said a prayer for Father, and did the shopping. If the afternoon was fine we either went for a walk in the country or a visit to Mother's great friend in the convent, Mother St Dominic. Mother had them all praying for Father, and every night, going to bed, I asked God to send him back safe from the war to us. Little, indeed, did I know what I was praying for!

One morning I got into the big bed, and there, sure enough, was Father in his usual Santa Claus manner, but later, instead of uniform, he put on his best blue suit, and Mother was as pleased as anything. I saw nothing to be pleased about, because, out of uniform, Father was altogether less interesting, but she only beamed, and explained that our prayers had been answered, and off we went to Mass to thank God for having brought Father safely home.

The irony of it! That very day when he came in to dinner he took off his boots and put on his slippers, donned the dirty old cap he wore about the house to save him from colds, crossed his legs, and began to talk gravely to Mother, who looked anxious. Naturally, I disliked her looking anxious, because it destroyed her good looks, so I interrupted him.

'Just a moment, Larry!' she said gently.

This was only what she said when we had boring visitors, so I attached no importance to it and went on talking.

'Do be quiet, Larry!' she said impatiently. 'Don't you hear me talking to Daddy?'

This was the first time I had heard those ominous words, 'talking to Daddy', and I couldn't help feeling that if this was how God answered prayers, he couldn't listen to them very attentively.

'Why are you talking to Daddy?' I asked with as great a show of indifference as I could muster.

'Because Daddy and I have business to discuss. Now don't interrupt again!'

In the afternoon, at Mother's request, Father took me for a walk. This time we went into town instead of out to the country, and I thought at first, in my usual optimistic way, that it might be an improvement. It was nothing of the sort. Father and I had quite different notions of a walk in town. He had no proper interest in trams, ships, and horses, and the only thing that seemed to divert him was talking to fellows as old as himself. When I wanted to stop he simply went on, dragging me behind him by the hand; when he wanted to stop I had no alternative but to do the same. I noticed that it seemed to be a sign that he wanted to stop for a long time whenever he leaned against a wall. The second time I saw him do it I got wild. He seemed to be settling himself forever. I pulled him by the coat and trousers, but, unlike Mother who, if you were too persistent, got into a wax and said: 'Larry, if you don't behave yourself, I'll give you a good slap,' Father had an extraordinary capacity for amiable inattention. I sized him up and wondered would I cry, but he seemed to be too remote to be annoyed even by that. Really, it was like going for a walk with a mountain! He either ignored the wrenching and pummelling entirely, or else glanced down with a grin of amusement from his peak. I had never met anyone so absorbed in himself as he seemed.

At teatime, 'talking to Daddy' began again, complicated this time by the fact that he had an evening paper, and every few minutes he put it down and told Mother something new out of it. I felt this was foul play. Man for man, I was prepared to compete with him any time for Mother's attention, but when he had it all made up for him by other people it left me no chance. Several times I tried to change the subject without success.

'You must be quiet while Daddy is reading, Larry,' Mother said impatiently.

It was clear that she either genuinely liked talking to Father better than talking to me, or else that he had some terrible hold on her which made her afraid to admit the truth.

'Mummy,' I said that night when she was tucking me up, 'do you think if I prayed hard God would send Daddy back to the war?'

She seemed to think about that for a moment.

'No, dear,' she said with a smile. 'I don't think he would.'

'Why wouldn't he, Mummy?'

'Because there isn't a war any longer, dear.'

'But, Mummy, couldn't God make another war, if He liked?'

'He wouldn't like to, dear. It's not God who makes wars, but bad people.'

'Oh!' I said.

I was quite disappointed about that. I began to think that God wasn't quite what he was cracked up to be.

Next morning I woke at my usual hour, feeling like a bottle of champagne. I put out my feet and invented a long conversation in which Mrs Right talked of the trouble she had with her own father till she put him in the Home. I didn't quite know what the Home was but it sounded the right place for Father. Then I got my chair and stuck my head out of the attic window. Dawn was just breaking, with a guilty air that made me feel I had caught it in the act. My head bursting with stories and schemes, I stumbled in next door, and in the half-darkness scrambled into the big bed. There was no room at Mother's side so I had to get between her and Father. For the time being I had forgotten about him, and for several minutes I sat bolt upright, racking my brains to know what I could do with him. He was taking up more than his fair share of the bed, and I couldn't get comfortable, so I gave him several kicks that made him grunt and stretch. He made room all right, though. Mother waked and felt for me. I settled back comfortably in the warmth of the bed with my thumb in my mouth.

'Mummy!' I hummed, loudly and contentedly.

'Sssh! dear,' she whispered. 'Don't wake Daddy!'

This was a new development, which threatened to be even more serious than 'talking to Daddy'. Life without my early-morning conferences was unthinkable.

'Why?' I asked severely.

'Because poor Daddy is tired.'

This seemed to me a quite inadequate reason, and I was sickened by the sentimentality of her 'poor Daddy'. I never liked that sort of gush; it always struck me as insincere.

'Oh!' I said lightly. Then in my most winning tone: 'Do you know where I want to go with you today, Mummy?'

'No, dear,' she sighed.

'I want to go down the Glen and fish for thornybacks with my new net, and then I want to go out to the Fox and Hound, and – '

'Don't-wake-Daddy!' she hissed angrily, clapping her hand across my mouth.

But it was too late. He was awake, or nearly so. He grunted and reached for the matches. Then he stared incredulously at his watch.

'Like a cup of tea, dear?' asked Mother in a meek, hushed voice I had never heard her use before. It sounded almost as though she were afraid.

'Tea?' he exclaimed indignantly. 'Do you know what the time is?'

'And after that I want to go up the Rathcooney Road,' I said loudly, afraid I'd forget something in all those interruptions.

'Go to sleep at once, Larry!' she said sharply.

I began to snivel. I couldn't concentrate, the way that pair went on, and smothering my early-morning schemes was like burying a family from the cradle.

Father said nothing, but lit his pipe and sucked it, looking out into the shadows without minding Mother or me. I knew he was mad. Every time I made a remark Mother hushed me irritably. I was mortified. I felt it wasn't fair; there was even something sinister in it. Every time I pointed out to her the waste of making two beds when we could both sleep in one, she had told me it was healthier like that, and now here was this man, this stranger, sleeping with her without the least regard for her health!

He got up early and made tea, but though he brought Mother a cup he brought none for me.

'Mummy,' I shouted, 'I want a cup of tea, too.'

'Yes, dear,' she said patiently. 'You can drink from Mummy's saucer.'

That settled it. Either Father or I would have to leave the house. I didn't want to drink from Mother's saucer; I wanted to be treated as an equal in my own home, so, just to spite her, I drank it all and left none for her. She took that quietly, too.

But that night when she was putting me to bed she said gently:

'Larry, I want you to promise me something.'

'What is it?' I asked.

'Not to come in and disturb poor Daddy in the morning. Promise?'

'Poor Daddy' again! I was becoming suspicious of everything involving that quite impossible man.

'Why?' I asked.

'Because poor Daddy is worried and tired and he doesn't sleep well.'

'Why doesn't he, Mummy?'

'Well, you know, don't you, that while he was at the war Mummy got the pennies from the Post Office?'

'From Miss MacCarthy?'

'That's right. But now, you see, Miss MacCarthy hasn't any more pennies, so Daddy must go out and find us some. You know what would happen if he couldn't?'

'No,' I said, 'tell us.'

'Well, I think we might have to go out and beg for them like the poor old woman on Fridays. We wouldn't like that, would we?'

'No,' I agreed. 'We wouldn't.'

'So you promise not to come in and wake him?'

'Promise.'

Mind you, I meant that. I knew pennies were a serious matter, and I was all against having to go out and beg like the old woman on Fridays. Mother laid out all my toys in a complete ring round the bed so that, whatever way I got out, I was bound to fall over one of them.

When I woke I remembered my promise all right. I got up and sat on the floor and played – for hours, it seemed to me. Then I got my chair and looked out of the attic window for more hours. I wished it was time for Father to wake; I wished someone would make me a cup of tea. I didn't feel in the least like the sun; instead I was bored and so very, very cold! I simply longed for the warmth and depth of the big featherbed.

At last I could stand it no longer. I went into the next room. As there was still no room at Mother's side I climbed over her and she woke with a start.

'Larry,' she whispered, gripping my arm very tightly, 'what did you promise?'

'But I did, Mummy,' I wailed, caught in the very act. 'I was quiet for ever so long.'

'Oh, dear, and you're perished!' she said sadly, feeling me all over. 'Now, if I let you stay will you promise not to talk?'

'But I want to talk, Mummy,' I wailed.

'That has nothing to do with it,' she said with a firmness that was new to me. 'Daddy wants to sleep. Now, do you understand that?'

I understood it only too well. I wanted to talk, he wanted to sleep – whose house was it, anyway?

'Mummy,' I said with equal firmness, 'I think it would be healthier for Daddy to sleep in his own bed.'

That seemed to stagger her, because she said nothing for a while.

'Now, once for all,' she went on, 'you're to be perfectly quiet or go back to your own bed. Which is it to be?'

The injustice of it got me down. I had convicted her out of her own mouth of inconsistency and unreasonableness, and she hadn't even attempted to reply. Full of spite, I gave Father a kick, which she didn't notice but which made him grunt and open his eyes in alarm.

'What time is it?' he asked in a panic-stricken voice, not looking at Mother but at the door, as if he saw someone there.

'It's early yet,' she replied soothingly. 'It's only the child. Go to sleep again . . . Now, Larry,' she added, getting out of bed, 'you've wakened Daddy and you must go back.'

This time, for all her quiet air, I knew she meant it, and knew that my principal rights and privileges were as good as lost unless I asserted them at once. As she lifted me, I gave a screech, enough to wake the dead, not to mind Father. He groaned.

'That damn child! Doesn't he ever sleep?'

'It's only a habit, dear,' she said quietly, though I could see she was vexed.

'Well, it's time he got out of it,' shouted Father, beginning to heave in the bed. He suddenly gathered all the bedclothes about him, turned to the wall and then looked back over his shoulder with nothing showing, only two small, spiteful, dark eyes. The man looked very wicked.

To open the bedroom door, Mother had to let me down, and I broke free and dashed for the farthest corner, screeching. Father sat bolt upright in bed.

'Shut up, you little puppy!' he said in a choking voice.

I was so astonished that I stopped screeching. Never, never had anyone spoken to me in that tone before. I looked at him incredulously and saw his face convulsed with rage. It was only then that I fully realized how God had **codded** me, listening to my prayers for the safe return of this monster.

'Shut up, you!' I bawled, beside myself.

'What's that you said?' shouted Father, making a wild leap out of the bed.

'Mick, Mick!' cried Mother. 'Don't you see the child isn't used to you?'

'I see he's better fed than taught,' snarled Father, waving his arms wildly. 'He wants his bottom smacked.'

All his previous shouting was as nothing to these obscene words referring to my person. They really made my blood boil.

'Smack your own!' I screamed hysterically. 'Smack your own! Shut up! Shut up!'

At this he lost his patience and let fly at me. He did it with the lack of conviction you'd expect of a man under Mother's horrified eyes, and it ended up as a mere tap, but the sheer indignity of being struck at all by a stranger, a total stranger who had cajoled his way back from the war into our big bed as a result of my innocent **intercession**, made me completely dotty. I shrieked and shrieked, and danced in my bare feet, and Father, looking awkward and hairy in nothing but a short grey army shirt, glared down at me like a mountain out for murder. I think it must have been then that I realised he was jealous too. And there stood

---

codded: deceived
intercession: prayer

Mother in her nightdress, looking as if her heart was broken between us. I hoped she felt as she looked. It seemed to me that she deserved it all.

From that morning out my life was a hell. Father and I were enemies, open and avowed. We conducted a series of skirmishes against one another, he trying to steal my time with Mother and I his. When she was sitting on my bed, telling me a story, he took to looking for some pair of old boots which he alleged he had left behind him at the beginning of the war. While he talked to Mother I played loudly with my toys to show my total lack of concern. He created a terrible scene one evening when he came in from work and found me at his box, playing with his regimental badges, Gurkha knives, and button-sticks. Mother got up and took the box from me.

'You mustn't play with Daddy's toys unless he lets you, Larry,' she said severely. 'Daddy doesn't play with yours.'

For some reason Father looked at her as if she had struck him and then turned away with a scowl.

'Those are not toys,' he growled, taking down the box again to see had I lifted anything. 'Some of those curios are very rare and valuable.'

But as time went on I saw more and more how he managed to **alienate** Mother and me. What made it worse was that I couldn't grasp his method or see what attraction he had for Mother. In every possible way he was less winning than I. He had a common accent and made noises at his tea. I thought for a while that it might be the newspapers she was interested in, so I made up bits of news of my own to read to her. Then I thought it might be the smoking, which I personally thought attractive, and took pipes and went round the house dribbling into them till he caught me. I even made noises at my tea, but Mother only told me I was disgusting. It all

---

alienate: separate

seemed to hinge round that unhealthy habit of sleeping together, so I made a point of dropping into their bedroom and nosing round, talking to myself, so that they wouldn't know I was watching them, but they were never up to anything that I could see. In the end it beat me. It seemed to depend on being grown-up and giving people rings, and I realized I'd have to wait.

But at the same time I wanted him to see that I was only waiting, not giving up the fight. One evening when he was being particularly obnoxious, chattering away well above my head, I let him have it.

'Mummy,' I said, 'do you know what I'm going to do when I grow up?'

'No, dear,' she replied. 'What?'

'I'm going to marry you,' I said quietly.

Father gave a great guffaw out of him, but he didn't take me in. I knew it must only be pretence. And Mother, in spite of everything, was pleased. I felt she was probably relieved to know that one day Father's hold on her would be broken.

'Won't that be nice?' she said with a smile.

'It will be very nice,' I said confidently. 'Because we're going to have lots and lots of babies.'

'That's right, dear,' she said placidly. 'I think we'll have one soon, and then you'll have plenty of company.'

I was no end pleased about that because it showed that in spite of the way she gave in to Father she still considered my wishes. Besides, it would put the Geneys in their place.

It didn't turn out like that, though. To begin with, she was very preoccupied – I supposed about where she would get the seventeen and six – and though Father took to staying out late in the evenings it did me no particular good. She stopped taking me for walks, became as touchy as blazes, and smacked me for nothing at all. Sometimes I wished I'd never mentioned the confounded baby – I seemed to have a genius for bringing calamity on myself.

And calamity it was! Sonny arrived in the most appalling hullabaloo – even that much he couldn't do without a fuss – and from the first moment I disliked him. He was a difficult child – so far as I was concerned he was always difficult – and demanded far too much attention. Mother was simply silly about him, and couldn't see when he was only showing off. As company he was worse than useless. He slept all day, and I had to go round the house on tiptoe to avoid waking him. It wasn't any longer a question of not waking Father. The slogan now was 'Don't-wake-Sonny!' I couldn't understand why the child wouldn't sleep at the proper time, so whenever Mother's back was turned I woke him. Sometimes to keep him awake I pinched him as well. Mother caught me at it one day and gave me a most unmerciful **flaking**.

One evening, when Father was coming in from work, I was playing trains in the front garden. I let on not to notice him; instead, I pretended to be talking to myself, and said in a loud voice: 'If another bloody baby comes into this house, I'm going out.'

Father stopped dead and looked at me across his shoulder.

'What's that you said?' he asked sternly.

'I was only talking to myself,' I replied, trying to conceal my panic. 'It's private.'

He turned and went in without a word. Mind you, I intended it as a solemn warning, but its effect was quite different. Father started being quite nice to me. I could understand that, of course. Mother was quite sickening about Sonny. Even at meal-times she'd get up and gawk at him in the cradle with an idiotic smile, and tell Father to do the same. He was always polite about it, but he looked

---

flaking: beating

so puzzled you could see he didn't know what she was talking about. He complained of the way Sonny cried at night, but she only got cross and said that Sonny never cried except when there was something up with him – which was a flaming lie, because Sonny never had anything up with him, and only cried for attention. It was really painful to see how simple-minded she was. Father wasn't attractive, but he had a fine intelligence. He saw through Sonny, and now he knew that I saw through him as well.

One night I woke with a start. There was someone beside me in the bed. For one wild moment I felt sure it must be Mother, having come to her senses and left Father for good, but then I heard Sonny in convulsions in the next room, and Mother saying: 'There! There! There!' and I knew it wasn't she. It was Father. He was lying beside me, wide awake, breathing hard and apparently as mad as hell.

After a while it came to me what he was mad about. It was his turn now. After turning me out of the big bed, he had been turned out himself. Mother had no consideration now for anyone but that poisonous pup, Sonny. I couldn't help feeling sorry for Father. I had been through it all myself, and even at that age I was **magnanimous**. I began to stroke him down and say: 'There! There!' He wasn't exactly responsive.

'Aren't you asleep either?' he snarled.

'Ah, come on and put your arm around us, can't you?' I said, and he did, in a sort of way. Gingerly, I suppose, is how you'd describe it. He was very bony but better than nothing.

At Christmas he went out of his way to buy me a really nice model railway.

---

magnanimous: generous, kindly

Getting Away From It All
Ann Walsh

The rats came the first night. She had seen their signs in the cabin when she unlocked the door and, trying to hide her own revulsion, had persuaded the children to sweep up the droppings and tufts of cotton pulled from the upholstered couch. By the time she had, according to the real estate lady's instructions, activated the propane appliances, pumped up the cistern that supplied running water, and disposed of the two full saucers of rat poison, the girls had finished their attempt at sweeping. It was clean enough for now she thought. Tomorrow she would sweep again, and mop the floor with a strong bleach solution. Exhausted by the long drive and the search for the isolated cabin she had rented for the summer, she tucked the girls firmly into their sleeping bags in one bedroom, settled herself in the other, and fell into a deep, dreamless sleep.

She should have realised, she told herself the next morning, she should have realised that the rats would come back. The groceries she had left stacked on the kitchen counter were scattered on the floor; loose macaroni mixing with rice, sugar and corn flakes. Every box, every bag, every item she had so carefully packed had been damaged in some way. Even less edible items – soap, pepper, paper towels – had been savaged, and fresh black droppings lay over everything like a satanic snowfall.

She cleaned up and, by the time the children woke, the kitchen showed no sign of the invasion. Everything was stored in the oven, the fridge, or sealer jars she had found in a cupboard, and she had discovered a large box of rat poison and refilled the saucers.

The cabin had been abandoned for several years, which was why the rent was within her single-parent budget. A faded 'For Sale' sign hung crookedly on a tree outside, mutely pleading for new owners. It was not far from a small town, but the access road, eleven miles of deeply-rutted, treacherous trail, had probably discouraged buyers.

Around the cabin the weeds were waist high, and she had to carry the four-year-old as they struggled down to the beach. A patch of scorched earth marked a firepit and a picnic table stood nearby, almost hidden in a thick stand of purple fireweed.

'Mummy?' Jenny's voice, usually strident with first-grade enthusiasm, was soft, timid. 'Do we have to stay in this place? I don't think I like it here.'

'Nonsense, Jen. It's just overgrown, lonely. No one has taken care of it for a long time. We'll clear a nice path down to the beach – see, there is a bit of a path under the weeds – then it will be easier for you to walk. We can build a campfire tonight and have hot dogs and marshmallows. It will be fun!' She smiled at the child, wondering why her own voice had sounded so loud and harsh.

The beach was beautiful; sandy and shallow for a long way out and nestled in a small cove that kept the water calm and warm. While the children splashed and searched for frogs, she began clearing the trail with a rusty, but still serviceable, sickle she found near the picnic table.

Once, stopping work to wipe the sweat from her eyes and to check on the children, she glanced up the hillside behind her and saw, almost hidden among tall cedars, the dark bulk of another, larger, cabin.

Curious, for no one had mentioned a second place close by, she called to the girls to stay out of the water until she came back, and pushed through the deep undergrowth on the hillside towards the hidden cabin.

It was large, built of grey-weathered logs, and surrounded by a wooden porch with a low railing. As she got closer, she could see that it was obviously deserted, and had been for a long time. The windows were boarded over with plywood, the steps to the front porch were pushed askew by saplings that nudged the foundations, and two solid planks were nailed, cross-like, over the front door. Oddly disappointed, she turned, and began the downward climb. As she walked, she realised why the large cabin had been built so far away from the water. The view was spectacular. She could see far across the lake, around a bend in the shore, to where a solitary mountain, still snow-capped in July, reared distantly through the heat haze. Below her the lake threw off slices of sunlight, and she could see her children digging intently in the sand. Of her own cabin, she glimpsed only the roof and her bedroom window through the trees.

In the evening, sunburned and exhausted, the girls again crawled into bed early. She made herself a cup of tea and with it walked down the now cleared path to the beach, admiring her handiwork. She stayed until the sun began to set, watching the coloured rays slant off the water then, tired herself, she made her way back up the trail.

When she reached the cabin, both children were crying. She ran to their room, stopping abruptly as a large grey rat sitting between the two beds slowly turned, stared at her for a moment with basalt eyes, then scurried between her legs and out of the door.

She reassured the children, set out yet another saucer of poison, and went to bed. That night she dreamed that she heard music.

Slowly, the cabin became home. The rats stayed away, although the poisoned bait seemed untouched. The sickle and an old push-mower revealed a tiny lawn, and the appearance of pansies alerted her to the presence of a flower bed edged with white-painted rocks. She took out several years' growth of weeds and discovered other perennials – pinks, day lilies and a clump of flowering poppies. Someone had once spent a great deal of time in this place, she thought. The propane stove, fridge and hot water heater, the fully operational bathroom and ingenious water supply, the flower beds and the pleasant, solid furniture all suggested a 'home' rather than just a summer cabin. A home that someone had loved, but left. 'Why?' she wondered, but quickly pushed the thought aside. Now it was her home; at least for a while. The children were happy; their bodies becoming tanned, their hair sun-streaked. The treasures of lake and forest, new to city children – minnows, frogs, chipmunks and the small kayak they had found – were keeping them cheerfully occupied. She was happy, too, she realised. Content. At peace.

But by the end of the first week in the cabin she was no longer sleeping well. The music that she heard in her dreams became louder, more persistent. There were party sounds too – the clink of glasses, distant bursts of laughter, sudden spatterings of conversations that she couldn't quite understand. Her dreams were always the same; she was lying in the narrow cot in the cabin and angrily listening to the sounds of a party to which she was not invited.

Then one night she realised that she wasn't asleep, wasn't dreaming! She sat up, fully awake, and listened. The music still played, the faint voices laughed. She went to the bedroom window, pushed aside the curtain, and stared out into the night. The big cabin on the hill glowed with light. It streamed through the large front windows, over the porch, touching the cedars with colour. Shadows moved against the windows and the music seemed louder.

Puzzled, she let the curtains fall back into place and went into the kitchen. She lit the lamps, made tea, and tried to laugh at herself and her sudden fear. The owners of the large cabin had come back and she, being so involved with the children, the lake, the flowers, hadn't noticed them arriving, that was all. But wouldn't she or the children have heard a car? Several cars in fact? And there was no road up the hill to the big cabin. Well, maybe there was another road, one she hadn't noticed. They could have come that way, perhaps.

But . . . the plywood had been removed from the windows, the front door was open, unbarred. Surely she would have heard hammering, shouts, the noises of opening a house that has been abandoned for a long time.

She stayed there in the bright kitchen until dawn came, listening to the sounds that faded with the growing light. When the sun dimmed the propane lights and tentatively reached across the room, she stood up and went outside. Uneasily, but with a growing sense of anticipation, she made her way through the long, early morning shadows, up the hill, towards the large, now silent, cabin.

Nothing had changed since she had last seen it. The boarded-over windows and doors, the saplings and weeds pushed against the porch and stairs and the thick, undisturbed underbrush on all sides were just as she had first seen them.

After that, she didn't try to sleep, but spent all her nights in the kitchen, turning the pages of a book, drinking tea, trying not to listen to the voices she knew she could not be hearing.

The twelfth night she heard them call her name.

The tourists were American, elderly, and kind. They pulled their big car onto the shoulder of the country road and spoke to the two bedraggled children who stood there, holding hands and trying not to cry.

'Mummy went away,' said the oldest, rubbing at her eyes with a scratched, sunburned hand. 'For two whole days. We got scared so we walked to the road.'

'We got losted,' said the small one. 'And see, a big rat in the cabin bit me. But I didn't cry.'

She held out her arm, proudly. The tourists looked at each other, their eyes wide with some unspeakable thought, then bundled the children into the car, turned around, and drove hurriedly back to the town they had just passed.

For on the child's arm was the perfect imprint of a vicious bite – two deep half-circles, the unmistakable mark left only by human teeth.

Star Light
Isaac Asimov

Arthur Trent heard them quite clearly. The tense, angry words shot out of his receiver.

'Trent! You can't get away. We will intersect your orbit in two hours and if you try to resist we will blow you out of space.'

Trent smiled and said nothing. He had no weapons and no need to fight. In far less than two hours the ship would make its jump through **hyperspace** and they would never find him. He would have with him nearly a kilogram of Krillium, enough for the construction of the brain-paths of thousands of robots and worth some ten million credits on any world in the Galaxy – and no questions asked.

Old Brennmeyer had planned the whole thing. He had planned it for thirty years and more. It had been his life's work.

'It's the getaway, young man,' he had said. 'That's why I need you. You can lift a ship off the ground and get out into space. I can't.'

'Getting it into space is no good, Mr Brennmeyer,' Trent said. 'We'll be caught in half a day.'

'Not,' said Brennmeyer, craftily, 'if we make **the Jump**; not if we flash through and end up light-years away.'

'It would take half a day to plot the Jump and even if we could take the time, the police would alert all stellar systems.'

'No, Trent, no.' The old man's hand fell on his, clutching it in trembling excitement. 'Not *all* stellar

---

hyperspace: space beyond the known universe
the Jump: the crossing over into another stellar system

systems; only the dozen in our neighbourhood. The Galaxy is big and the colonists of the last fifty thousand years have lost touch with each other.'

He talked avidly, painting the picture. The Galaxy now was like the surface of man's original planet (Earth, they had called it) in prehistoric times. Man had been scattered over all the continents, but each group had known only the area immediately surrounding itself.

'If we make the Jump at random,' Brennmeyer said, 'we would be anywhere, even fifty thousand light-years away, and there would be no more chance of finding us than a pebble in a meteor swarm.'

Trent shook his head. 'And we don't find ourselves, either. We wouldn't have the foggiest way of getting to an inhabited planet.'

Brennmeyer's quick-moving eyes inspected the surroundings. No one was near him, but his voice sank to a whisper anyway. 'I've spent thirty years collecting data on every habitable planet in the Galaxy. I've searched all the old records. I've travelled thousands of light-years, farther than any space-pilot. And the location of every habitable planet is now in the memory store of the best computer in the world.'

Trent lifted his eyebrows politely.

Brennmeyer said, 'I design computers and I have the best. I've also plotted the exact location of every luminous star in the Galaxy, every star of spectral class of F, B, A, and O, and put that into the memory store. Once we've made the Jump the computer will scan the heavens spectroscopically and compare the results with the map of the Galaxy it contains. Once it finds the proper match, and sooner or later it will, the ship is located in space and it is then automatically guided through a second Jump to the neighbourhood of the nearest inhabited planet.'

'Sounds too complicated.'

'It can't miss. All these years I've worked on it and it can't miss. I'll have ten years left to be a millionaire. But you're young; you'll be a millionaire much longer.'

'When you Jump at random, you can end inside a star.'

'Not one chance in a hundred trillion, Trent. We might also land so far from any luminous star that the computer can't find anything to match up against its programme. We might find we've jumped only a light-year or two and the police are still on our trail. The chances of that are smaller still. If you want to worry, worry that you might die of a heart attack at the moment of take-off. The chances for that are much higher.'

'*You* might, Mr Brennmeyer. You're older.'

The old man shrugged. 'I don't count. The computer will do everything automatically.'

Trent nodded and remembered that. One midnight, when the ship was ready and Brennmeyer arrived with the Krillium in a briefcase (he had no difficulty, for he was a greatly trusted man) Trent took the briefcase with one hand while his other moved quickly and surely.

A knife was still the best, just as quick as a molecular depolariser, just as fatal, and much more quiet. Trent left the knife there with the body, complete with fingerprints. What was the difference? They wouldn't get him.

Deep in space now, with the police-cruisers in pursuit, he felt the gathering tension that always preceded a Jump. No physiologist could explain it, but every space-wise pilot knew what it felt like.

There was a momentary inside-out feeling as his ship and himself for one moment of non-space and non-time, became non-matter and non-energy, then reassembled itself instantaneously in another part of the Galaxy.

Trent smiled. He was still alive. No star was too close and there were thousands that were close enough. The sky was alive with stars and the pattern was so different that he knew the Jump had gone far. Some of those stars had to be spectral class F and better. The computer would have a nice, rich pattern to match against its memory. It shouldn't take long.

He leaned back in comfort and watched the bright pattern of starlight move as the ship rotated slowly. A bright star came into view, a really bright one. It didn't seem more than a couple of light-years away and his pilot's sense told him it was a hot one; good and hot. The computer would use that as its base and match the pattern centred about it. Once again, he thought: It shouldn't take long.

But it did. The minutes passed. Then an hour. And still the computer clicked busily and its lights flashed.

Trent frowned. Why didn't it find the pattern? The pattern had to be there. Brennmeyer had showed him his long years of work. He *couldn't* have left out a star or recorded it in the wrong place.

Surely stars were born and died and moved through space while in being, but these changes were slow, slow. In a million years, the patterns that Brennmeyer had recorded couldn't –

A sudden panic clutched at Trent. No! It *couldn't* be. The chances for it were even smaller than Jumping into a star's interior.

He waited for the bright star to come into view again, and, with trembling hands, brought it into telescopic focus. He put in all the magnification he could, and around the bright speck of light was the tell-tale fog of turbulent gases caught, as it were, in mid-flight.

*It was a **nova**!*

From dim obscurity, the star had raised itself to bright luminosity – perhaps only a month ago. It had graduated from a special class low enough to be ignored by

---

nova: a new star

the computer, to one that would be most certainly taken into account.

But the nova that existed in space didn't exist in the computer's memory store because Brennmeyer had not put it there. It had not existed when Brennmeyer was collecting his data – at least not as a luminous star.

'Don't count on it,' shrieked Trent. 'Ignore it.'

But he was shouting at automatic machinery that would match the nova-centred pattern against the Galactic pattern and find it nowhere and continue, nevertheless, to match and match and match for as long as its energy supply held out.

The air supply would run out much sooner. Trent's life would ebb away much sooner.

Helplessly, Trent slumped in his chair, watching the mocking pattern of star light and beginning the long and agonised wait for death.

– If he had only kept the knife.

Reunion
Arthur C Clarke

People of Earth, do not be afraid. We come in peace –
and why not? For we are your cousins; we have been
here before.

You will recognise us when we meet, a few hours from
now. We are approaching the solar system almost as quickly
as this radio message. Already, your sun dominates the sky
ahead of us. It is the sun our ancestors and yours shared ten
million years ago. We are men, as you are; but you have
forgotten your history, while we have remembered ours.

We colonized Earth, in the reign of the great reptiles,
who were dying when we came and whom we could not
save. Your world was a tropical planet then, and we felt
that it would make a fair home for our people. We were
wrong. Though we were masters of space, we knew so
little about climate, about evolution, about genetics . . .

For millions of summers – there were no winters in
those ancient days – the colony flourished. Isolated
though it had to be, in a universe where the journey from
one star to the next takes years, it kept in touch with its
parent civilization. Three or four times in every century,
starships would call and bring news of the galaxy.

But two million years ago, Earth began to change.
For ages it had been a tropical paradise; then the
temperature fell, and the ice began to creep down from
the poles. As the climate altered, so did the colonists. We
realize now that it was a natural adaptation to the end of
the long summer, but those who had made Earth their
home for so many generations believed that they had
been attacked by a strange and repulsive disease. A
disease that did not kill, that did no physical harm – but
merely disfigured.

Yet some were immune; the change spared them and their children. And so, within a few thousand years, the colony had split into two separate groups – almost two separate species – suspicious and jealous of each other.

The division brought envy, discord, and, ultimately, conflict. As the colony disintegrated and the climate steadily worsened, those who could do so withdrew from Earth. The rest sank into barbarism.

We could have kept in touch, but there is so much to do in a universe of a hundred trillion stars. Until a few years ago, we did not know that any of you had survived. Then we picked up your first radio signals, learned your simple languages, and discovered that you had made the long climb back from savagery. We come to greet you, our long-lost relatives – and to help you.

We have discovered much in the eons since we abandoned Earth. If you wish us to bring back the eternal summer that ruled before the Ice Ages, we can do so. Above all, we have a simple remedy for the offensive yet harmless genetic plague that afflicted so many of the colonists.

Perhaps it has run its course – but if not, we have good news for you. People of Earth, you can rejoin the society of the universe without shame, without embarrassment.

If any of you are still white, we can cure you.

The Doll's House
Katherine Mansfield

When dear old Mrs Hay went back to town after staying with the Burnells she sent the children a doll's house. It was so big that the **carter** and Pat carried it into the courtyard, and there it stayed, propped up on two wooden boxes beside the feed-room door. No harm could come to it; it was summer. And perhaps the smell of paint would have gone off it by the time it had to be taken in. For really, the smell of paint coming from that doll's house ('Sweet of old Mrs Hay, of course; most sweet and generous!') – but the smell of paint was enough to make anyone seriously ill, in Aunt Beryl's opinion. Even before the sacking was taken off. And when it was . . .

There stood the doll's house, a dark, oily, spinach green, picked out with bright yellow. Its two solid little chimneys, glued on to the roof, were painted red and white, and the door, gleaming with yellow varnish, was like a little slab of toffee. Four windows, real windows, were divided into panes by a broad streak of green. There was actually a tiny porch, too, painted yellow, with big lumps of congealed paint hanging along the edge.

But perfect, perfect little house! Who could possibly mind the smell? It was part of the joy, part of the newness.

'Open it quickly, someone!'

The hook at the side was fast. Pat prised it open with his penknife, and the whole house front swung back, and – there you were, gazing at one and the same moment into the drawing-room and the dining-room, the kitchen and two bedrooms. That is the way for a house to open!

---

carter: delivery man

Why don't all houses open like that? How much more exciting than peering through the slit of a door into a mean little hall with a hat-stand and two umbrellas! That is – isn't it? – what you long to know about a house when you put your hand on the knocker. Perhaps it is the way God opens houses at the dead of night when He is taking a quiet **turn** with an angel . . .

'Oh-oh!' The Burnell children sounded as if they were in despair. It was too marvellous; it was too much for them. They had never seen anything like it in their lives. All the rooms were papered. There were pictures on the walls, painted on the paper, with gold frames complete. Red carpet covered all the floors except the kitchen; red plush chairs in the drawing-room, green in the dining-room; tables, beds with real bedclothes, a cradle, a stove, a dresser with tiny plates and one big jug. But what Kezia liked more than anything, what she liked frightfully, was the lamp. It stood in the middle of the dining-room table, an exquisite little amber lamp for lighting, though, of course, you couldn't light it. But there was something inside that looked like oil and moved when you shook it.

The father and mother dolls, who sprawled very stiff as though they had fainted in the drawing-room, and their two little children asleep upstairs, were really too big for the doll's house. They didn't look as though they belonged. But the lamp was perfect. It seemed to smile at Kezia, to say, 'I live here'. The lamp was real.

The Burnell children could hardly walk to school fast enough the next morning. They burned to tell everybody, to describe, to – well – to boast about their doll's house before the school bell rang.

'I'm to tell,' said Isabel, 'because I'm the eldest. And you two can join in after. But I'm to tell first.'

---

turn: walk, stroll

There was nothing to answer. Isabel was bossy, but she was always right, and Lottie and Kezia knew too well the powers that went with being eldest. They brushed through the thick buttercups at the road edge and said nothing.

'And I'm to choose who's to come and see it first. Mother said I might.'

For it had been arranged that while the doll's house stood in the courtyard they might ask the girls at school, two at a time, to come and look. Not to stay to tea, of course, or to come traipsing through the house. But just to stand quietly in the courtyard while Isabel pointed out the beauties, and Lottie and Kezia looked pleased . . .

But hurry as they might, by the time they had reached the tarred palings of the boys' playground the bell had begun to jangle. They only just had time to whip off their hats and fall into line before the roll was called. Never mind. Isabel tried to make up for it by looking very important and mysterious and by whispering behind her hand to the girls near her, 'Got something to tell you at playtime'.

Playtime came and Isabel was surrounded. The girls of her class nearly fought to put their arms round her, to walk away with her, to beam flatteringly, to be her special friend. She **held quite a court** under the huge pine trees at the side of the playground. Nudging, giggling together, the little girls pressed up close. And the only two who stayed outside the ring were the two who were always outside, the little Kelveys. They knew better than to come anywhere near the Burnells.

For the fact was, the school the Burnell children went to was not at all the kind of place their parents would have chosen if there had been any choice. But there was none. It was the only school for miles. And the consequence was all the children of the neighbourhood,

---

held quite a court: acted like a queen

the Judge's little girls, the doctor's daughters, the store-keeper's children, the milkman's, were forced to mix together. Not to speak of there being an equal number of rude, rough little boys as well. But the line had to be drawn somewhere. It was drawn at the Kelveys. Many of the children, including the Burnells, were not allowed even to speak to them. They walked past the Kelveys with their heads in the air, and as they set the fashion in all matters of behaviour, the Kelveys were shunned by everybody. Even the teacher had a special voice for them, and a special smile for the other children when Lil Kelvey came up to the desk with a bunch of dreadfully common-looking flowers.

They were the daughters of a spry, hard-working little washerwoman, who went about from house to house by the day. This was awful enough. But where was Mr Kelvey? Nobody knew for certain. But everybody said he was in prison. So they were the daughters of a washerwoman and a gaolbird. Very nice company for other people's children! And they looked it. Why Mrs Kelvey made them so conspicuous was hard to understand. The truth was they were dressed in 'bits' given to her by the people for whom she worked. Lil, for instance, who was a stout, plain child, with big freckles, came to school in a dress made from a green **art-serge** tablecloth of the Burnells' with red plush sleeves from the Logans' curtains. Her hat, perched on top of her high forehead, was a grown-up woman's hat, once the property of Miss Lecky, the postmistress. It was turned up at the back and trimmed with a large scarlet quill. What a little **guy** she looked! It was impossible not to laugh. And her little sister, 'our Else', wore a long white dress, rather like a nightgown, and a pair of little boy's boots. But whatever our Else wore would have looked strange. She was a tiny wishbone of a child, with cropped

---

art-serge: fashionable silk
guy: fright

hair and enormous solemn eyes – a little white owl. Nobody had ever seen her smile; she scarcely ever spoke. She went through life holding on to Lil, with a piece of Lil's skirt screwed up in her hand. Where Lil went, our Else followed. In the playground, on the road, going to and from school, there was Lil marching in front and our Else holding on behind. Only when she wanted anything, or when she was out of breath, our Else gave Lil a tug, a twitch, and Lil stopped and turned round. The Kelveys never failed to understand each other.

Now they hovered at the edge; you couldn't stop them listening. When the little girls turned round and sneered, Lil, as usual, gave her silly, shamefaced smile, but our Else only looked.

And Isabel's voice, so very proud, went on telling. The carpet made a great sensation, but so did the beds with real bedclothes, and the stove with an oven door.

When she had finished, Kezia broke in. 'You've forgotten the little lamp, Isabel.'

'Oh yes', said Isabel, 'and there's a teeny little lamp, all made of yellow glass, with a white globe, that stands on the dining-room table. You couldn't tell it from a real one.'

'The lamp's best of all,' cried Kezia. She thought Isabel wasn't making half enough of the little lamp. But nobody paid any attention. Isabel was choosing the two who were to come back with them that afternoon and see it. She chose Emmie Cole and Lena Logan. But when the others knew they were all to have a chance, they couldn't be nice enough to Isabel. One by one they put their arms round Isabel's waist and walked her off. They had something to whisper to her, a secret. 'Isabel's *my* friend.'

Only the little Kelveys moved away, forgotten; there was nothing more for them to hear.

Days passed, and as more children saw the doll's house, the fame of it spread. It became the one subject, the rage. The one question was: 'Have you seen the Burnells' doll's house? Oh, ain't it lovely!' 'Haven't you seen it? Oh, I say!'

Even the dinner hour was given up to talking about it. The little girls sat under the pines eating their thick mutton sandwiches and big slabs of **johnny cake** spread with butter. While always, as near as they could get, sat the Kelveys, our Else holding on to Lil, listening too, while they chewed their jam sandwiches out of a newspaper soaked with large red blobs.

'Mother,' said Kezia, 'can I ask the Kelveys just once?'

'Certainly not, Kezia.'

'But why not?'

'Run away, Kezia; you know quite well why not.'

At last everybody had seen it except them. On that day the subject rather flagged. It was the dinner hour. The children stood together under the pine trees, and suddenly, as they looked at the Kelveys eating out of their paper, they wanted to be horrid to them. Emmie Cole started the whisper.

'Lil Kelvey's going to be a servant when she grows up.'

'O-oh, how awful!' said Isabel Burnell, and she made eyes at Emmie.

Emmie swallowed in a very meaning way and nodded to Isabel as she'd seen her mother do on these occasions.

'It's true – it's true – it's true,' she said.

Then Lena Logan's little eyes snapped. 'Shall I ask her?' she whispered.

'Bet you don't,' said Jessie May.

'Pooh – I'm not frightened,' said Lena. Suddenly she gave a little squeal and danced in front of the other girls. 'Watch! Watch me! Watch me now!' said Lena. And sliding, gliding, dragging one foot, giggling behind her hand, Lena went over to the Kelveys.

---

johnny cake: a cake made of maizemeal

Lil looked up from her dinner. She wrapped the rest quickly away. Our Else stopped chewing. What was coming now?

'Is it true you're going to be a servant when you grow up, Lil Kelvey?' shrilled Lena.

Dead silence. But instead of answering, Lil only gave her silly, shamefaced smile. She didn't seem to mind the question at all. What **a sell** for Lena! The girls began to titter.

Lena couldn't stand that. She put her hands on her hips; she shot forward. 'Yah, yer father's in prison!' she hissed spitefully.

This was such a marvellous thing to have said that the little girls rushed away in a body, deeply, deeply excited, wild with joy. Someone found a long rope, and they began skipping. And never did they skip so high, run in and out so fast, or do such daring things as on that morning.

In the afternoon Pat called for the Burnell children with the **buggy** and they drove home. There were visitors. Isabel and Lottie, who liked visitors, went upstairs to change their pinafores. But Kezia **thieved** out at the back. Nobody was about; she began to swing on the big white gates of the courtyard. Presently, looking along the road, she saw two little dots. They grew bigger, they were coming towards her. Now she could see that one was in front and one close behind. Now she could see that they were the Kelveys. Kezia stopped swinging. She slipped off the gate as if she was going to run away. Then she hesitated. The Kelveys came nearer, and beside them walked their shadows, very long in the buttercups. Kezia clambered back on the gate; she had made up her mind. She swung out.

---

a sell: a show-up
buggy: horse-drawn carriage
thieved: sneaked

'Hello,' she said to the passing Kelveys.

They were so astounded that they stopped. Lil gave her silly smile. Our Else stared.

'You can come and see our doll's house if you want to,' said Kezia, and she dragged one toe on the ground. But at that Lil turned red and shook her head quickly.

'Why not?' asked Kezia.

Lil gasped, then she said, 'Your ma told our ma you wasn't to speak to us.'

'Oh, well,' said Kezia. She didn't know what to reply. 'It doesn't matter. You can come and see our doll's house all the same. Come on. Nobody's looking.'

But Lil shook her head still harder.

'Don't you want to?' asked Kezia.

Suddenly there was a twitch, a tug at Lil's skirt. She turned round. Our Else was looking at her with big, imploring eyes; she was frowning; she wanted to go. For a moment Lil looked at our Else very doubtfully. But then our Else twitched her skirt again. She started forward. Kezia led the way. Like two stray cats they followed across the courtyard to where the doll's house stood.

'There it is,' said Kezia.

There was a pause. Lil breathed loudly, almost snorted; our Else was still as stone.

'I'll open it for you,' said Kezia kindly. She undid the hook and they looked inside.

'There's the drawing-room and the dining-room, and that's the – '

'Kezia!'

Oh, what a start they gave!

'Kezia!'

It was Aunt Beryl's voice. They turned round. At the back door stood Aunt Beryl, staring as if she couldn't believe what she saw.

'How dare you ask the little Kelveys into the courtyard!' said her cold, furious voice. 'You know as well as I do, you're not allowed to talk to them. Run away, children, run away at once. And don't come back again,' said Aunt Beryl. Then she stepped into the yard and shooed them out as if they were chickens.

'Off you go immediately!' she called, cold and proud.

They did not need telling twice. Burning with shame, shrinking together, Lil huddling along like her mother, our Else dazed, somehow they crossed the big courtyard and squeezed through the white gate.

'Wicked, disobedient little girl!' said Aunt Beryl bitterly to Kezia, and she slammed to doll's house to.

The afternoon had been awful. A letter had come from **Willie Brent**, a terrifying, threatening letter, saying if she did not meet him that evening in Pulman's Bush, he'd come to the front door and ask the reason why! But now that she had frightened those little rats of Kelveys and given Kezia a good scolding, her heart felt lighter. That ghastly pressure was gone. She went back to the house humming.

When the Kelveys were well out of sight of the Burnells', they sat down to rest on a big red drainpipe by the side of the road. Lil's cheeks were still burning; she took off the hat with the quill and held it on her knee. Dreamily they looked over the hay paddocks, past the creek, to the group of **wattles** where Logan's cows stood waiting to be milked. What were their thoughts?

Presently our Else nudged up close to her sister. But now she had forgotten the cross lady. She put out a finger and stroked her sister's quill; she smiled her rare smile.

'I seen the little lamp,' she said softly.

Then both were silent once more.

Willie Brent: Aunt Beryl's lover
wattles: wooden stakes

Through the Tunnel
Doris Lessing

Going to the shore on the first morning of the holiday, the young English boy stopped at a turning of the path and looked down at a wild and rocky bay, and then over to the crowded beach he knew so well from other years. His mother walked on in front of him, carrying a bright striped bag in one hand. Her other arm, swinging loose, was very white in the sun. The boy watched that white, naked arm, and turned his eyes, which had a frown behind them, towards the bay and back again to his mother. When she felt he was not with her, she swung around. 'Oh, there you are, Jerry!' she said. She looked impatient, then smiled. 'Why, darling, would you rather not come with me? Would you rather – ' She frowned, conscientiously worrying over what amusements he might secretly be longing for, which she had been too busy or too careless to imagine. He was very familiar with that anxious, apologetic smile. **Contrition** sent him running after her. And yet, as he ran, he looked back over his shoulder at the wild bay; and all morning, as he played on the safe beach, he was thinking of it.

Next morning, when it was time for the routine of swimming and sunbathing, his mother said, 'Are you tired of the usual beach, Jerry? Would you like to go somewhere else?'

'Oh, no!' he said quickly, smiling at her out of that unfailing impulse of contrition – a sort of chivalry. Yet, walking down the path with her, he blurted out, 'I'd like to go and have a look at those rocks down there.'

---

contrition: feeling sorry

She gave the idea her attention. It was a wild-looking place, and there was no one there; but she said, 'Of course, Jerry. When you've had enough, come to the big beach. Or just go straight back to the villa, if you like.' She walked away, that bare arm, now slightly reddened from yesterday's sun, swinging. And he almost ran after her again, feeling it unbearable that she should go by herself, but he did not.

She was thinking, Of course he's old enough to be safe without me. Have I been keeping him too close? He mustn't feel he ought to be with me. I must be careful.

He was an only child, eleven years old. She was a widow. She was determined to be neither possessive nor lacking in devotion. She went worrying off to her beach.

As for Jerry, once he saw that his mother had gained her beach, he began the steep descent to the bay. From where he was, high up among red-brown rocks, it was a scoop of moving bluish green fringed with white. As he went lower, he saw that it spread among small promontories and inlets of rough, sharp rock, and the crisping, lapping surface showed stains of purple and darker blue. Finally, as he ran sliding and scraping down the last few yards, he saw an edge of white surf and the shallow, luminous movement of water over white sand, and, beyond that, a solid heavy blue.

He ran straight into the water and began swimming. He was a good swimmer. He went out fast over the gleaming sand, over a middle region where rocks lay like discoloured monsters under the surface and then he was in the real sea – a warm sea where irregular cold currents from the deep water shocked his limbs.

When he was so far out that he could look back not only on the little bay but past the promontory that was between it and the big beach, he floated on the buoyant surface and looked for his mother. There she was, a speck of yellow under an umbrella that looked like a slice of orange peel. He swam back to shore, relieved at being sure she was there, but all at once very lonely.

On the edge of a small cape that marked the side of the bay away from the promontory was a loose scatter of rocks. Above them, some boys were stripping off their clothes. They came running, naked, down to the rocks. The English boy swam towards them, but kept his distance at a stone's throw. They were of that coast; all of them were burned smooth dark brown and speaking a language he did not understand. To be with them, of them, was a craving that filled his whole body. He swam a little closer; they turned and watched him with narrowed, alert dark eyes. Then one smiled and waved. It was enough. In a minute, he had swum in and was on the rocks beside then, smiling with a desperate, nervous **supplication**. They shouted cheerful greetings at him; and then, as he preserved his nervous, uncomprehending smile, they understood that he was a foreigner strayed from his own beach, and they proceeded to forget him. But he was happy. He was with them.

They began diving again and again from a high point into a well of blue sea between rough, pointed rocks. After they had dived and come up, they swam around, hauled themselves up, and waited their turn to dive again. They were big boys – men, to Jerry. He dived, and they watched him; and when he swam around to take his place, they made way for him. He felt he was accepted and he dived again, carefully, proud of himself.

Soon the biggest of the boys poised himself, shot down into the water, and did not come up. The others stood about, watching. Jerry, after waiting for the sleek brown head to appear, let out a yell of warning; they looked at him idly and turned their eyes back towards the water. After a long time, the boy came up on the other side of a

supplication: pleading

big dark rock, letting the air out of his lungs in a sputtering gasp and a shout of triumph. Immediately the rest of them dived in. One moment, the morning seemed full of chattering boys; the next, the air and the surface of the water were empty. But through the heavy blue, dark shapes could be seen moving and groping.

Jerry dived, shot past the school of underwater swimmers, saw a black wall of rock looming at him, touched it, and bobbed up at once to the surface, where the wall was a low barrier he could see across. There was no one visible; under him, in the water, the dim shapes of the swimmers had disappeared. Then one, and then another of the boys came up on the far side of the barrier of rock, and he understood that they had swum through some gap or hole in it. He plunged down again. He could see nothing through the stinging salt water but the blank rock. When he came up the boys were all on the diving rock, preparing to attempt the feat again. And now, in a panic of failure, he yelled up, in English, 'Look at me! Look!' and he began splashing and kicking in the water like a foolish dog.

They looked down gravely, frowning. He knew the frown. At moments of failure, when he clowned to claim his mother's attention, it was with just this grave, embarrassed inspection that she rewarded him. Through his hot shame, feeling the pleading grin on his face like a scar that he could never remove, he looked up at the group of big brown boys on the rock and shouted, *'Bonjour! Merci! Au revoir! Monsieur, monsieur!'* while he hooked his fingers round his ears and waggled them.

Water surged into his mouth; he choked, sank, came up. The rock, lately weighted with boys, seemed to rear up out of the water as their weight was removed. They were flying down past him now, into the water; the air was full of falling bodies. Then the rock was empty in the hot sunlight. He counted one, two, three . . .

At fifty, he was terrified. They must all be drowning beneath him, in the watery caves of the rock. At a hundred, he stared around him at the empty hillside, wondering if he should yell for help. He counted faster, faster, to hurry them up, to bring them to the surface quickly, to drown them quickly – anything rather than the terror of counting on and on into the blue emptiness of the morning. And then, at a hundred and sixty, the water beyond the rock was full of boys blowing like brown whales. They swam back to the shore without a look at him.

He climbed back to the diving rock and sat down, feeling the hot roughness of it under his thighs. The boys were gathering up their bits of clothing and running off along the shore to another promontory. They were leaving to get away from him. He cried openly, fists in his eyes. There was no one to see him, and he cried himself out.

It seemed to him that a long time had passed, and he swam out to where he could see his mother. Yes, she was still there, a yellow spot under an orange umbrella. He swam back to the big rock, climbed up, and dived into the blue pool among the fanged and angry boulders. Down he went, until he touched the wall of rock again. But the salt was so painful in his eyes that he could not see.

He came to the surface, swam to shore and went back to the villa to wait for his mother. Soon she walked slowly up the path, swinging her striped bag, the flushed, naked arm dangling beside her. 'I want some swimming goggles,' he panted, defiant and beseeching.

She gave him a patient, inquisitive look as she said casually, 'Well, of course, darling.'

But now, now, now! He must have them this minute, and no other time. He nagged and pestered until she went with him to a shop. As soon as she had bought the goggles, he grabbed them from her hand as if she were going to claim them for herself, and was off, running down the steep path to the bay.

Jerry swam out to the big barrier rock, adjusted the goggles, and dived. The impact of the water broke the rubber-enclosed vacuum, and the goggles came loose. He understood that he must swim down to the base of the rock from the surface of the water. He fixed the goggles tight and firm, filled his lungs, and floated, face down, on the water. Now, he could see. It was as if he had eyes of a different kind – fish eyes that showed everything clear and delicate and wavering in the bright water.

Under him, six or seven feet down, was a floor of perfectly clean, shining white sand, rippled firm and hard by the tides. Two greyish shapes steered there, like long, rounded pieces of wood or slate. They were fish. He saw them nose towards each other, poise motionless, make a dart forward, swerve off, and come around again. It was like a water dance. A few inches above them the water sparkled as if sequins were dropping through it. Fish again – myriads of minute fish, the length of his fingernail, were drifting through the water, and in moments he could feel the innumerable tiny touches of them against his limbs. It was like swimming in flaked silver. The great rock the big boys had swum through rose sheer out of the white sand – black, tufted lightly with greenish weed. He could see no gap in it. He swam down to its base.

Again and again he rose, took a big chestful of air, and went down again. Again and again he groped over the surface of the rock, feeling it, almost hugging it in the desperate need to find the entrance. And then, once, while he was clinging to the black wall, his knees came up and he shot his feet out forward and they met no obstacle. He had found the hole.

He gained the surface, clambered about the stones that littered the barrier rock until he found a big one, and, with this in his arms, let himself down over the side of the rock. He dropped, with the weight, straight to the sandy floor. Clinging tight to the anchor of stone, he lay on his side and looked in under the dark shelf at the place where his feet had gone. He could see the hole. It was an irregular, dark gap but he could not see deep into it. He let go of his anchor, clung with his hands to the edges of the hole, and tried to push himself in.

He got his head in, found his shoulders jammed, moved them in sideways, and was inside as far as his waist. He could see nothing ahead. Something soft and clammy touched his mouth; he saw a dark frond moving against the greyish rock, and panic filled him. He thought of octopuses, of clinging weed. He pushed himself out backwards and caught a glimpse, as he retreated, of a harmless tentacle of seaweed drifting in the mouth of the tunnel. But it was enough. He reached the sunlight, swam to shore, and lay on the diving rock. He looked down into the blue well of water. He knew he must find his way through that cave, or hole, or tunnel, and out the other side.

First, he thought, he must learn to control his breathing. He let himself down into the water with another big stone in his arms, so that he could lie effortlessly on the bottom of the sea. He counted. One, two, three. He counted steadily. He could hear the movement of blood in his chest. Fifty-one, fifty-two . . . His chest was hurting. He let go of the rock and went up into the air. He saw the sun was low. He rushed to the villa and found his mother at her supper. She said only, 'Did you enjoy yourself?' and he said, 'Yes.'

All night the boy dreamed of the water-filled cave in the rock, and as soon as breakfast was over he went to the bay.

That night, his nose bled badly. For hours he had been underwater, learning to hold his breath, and now he felt weak and dizzy. His mother said, 'I shouldn't overdo things, darling, if I were you.'

That day and the next, Jerry exercised his lungs as if everything, the whole of his life, all that he would become, depended upon it. Again his nose bled at night, and his mother insisted on his coming with her the next day. It was torment to him to waste a day of this careful self-training, but he stayed with her on that other beach, which now seemed a place for small children, a place where his mother might lie safe in the sun. It was not his beach.

He did not ask for permission, on the following day, to go to his beach. He went, before his mother could consider the complicated rights and wrongs of the matter. A day's rest, he discovered, had improved his count by ten. The big boys had made the passage while he counted a hundred and sixty. He had been counting fast, in his fright. Probably now, if he tried, he could get through that long tunnel, but he was not going to try yet. A curious, most unchildlike persistence, a controlled impatience, made him wait. In the meantime, he lay under water on the white sand, littered now by stones he had brought down from the upper air, and studied the entrance to the tunnel. He knew every jut and corner of it, as far as it was possible to see. It was as if he already felt its sharpness about his shoulders.

He sat by the clock in the villa, when his mother was not near, and checked his time. He was incredulous and then proud to find he could hold his breath without strain for two minutes. The words, 'two minutes', authorized by the clock, brought close the adventure that was so necessary to him.

In another four days, his mother said casually one morning, they must go home. On the day before they left, he would do it. He would do it if it killed him, he said defiantly to himself. But two days before they were to leave – a day of triumph when he increased his count by fifteen – his nose bled so badly that he turned dizzy and had to lie limply over the big rock like a bit of seaweed, watching the thick red blood flow on to the rock and trickle slowly down to the sea. He was frightened. Supposing he turned dizzy in the tunnel? Supposing he died there, trapped? Supposing – his head went around, in the hot sun, and he almost gave up. He thought he would return to the house and lie down, and next summer, perhaps, when he had another year's growth in him – *then* he would go through the hole.

But even after he had made the decision, or thought he had, he found himself sitting up on the rock and looking down into the water; and he knew that now, this moment, when his nose had only just stopped bleeding, when his head was still sore and throbbing – this was the moment when he would try. If he did not do it now, he never would. He was trembling with fear that he would not go; and he was trembling with horror at that long, long tunnel under the rock, under the sea. Even in the open sunlight, the barrier rock seemed very wide and very heavy; tons of rock pressed down on where he would go. If he died there, he would lie until one day – perhaps not before next year – those big boys would swim into it and find it blocked.

He put on his goggles, fitted them tight, tested the vacuum. His hands were shaking. Then he chose the biggest stone he could carry and slipped over the edge of the rock until half of him was in the cool, enclosing water and half in the hot sun. He looked up once at the empty sky, filled his lungs once, twice, and then sank fast to the bottom with the stone. He let it go and began to count. He took the edges of the hole in his hands and drew himself into it, wriggling his shoulders in sideways as he remembered he must, kicking himself along with his feet.

Soon he was clear inside. He was in a small rock-bound hole filled with yellowish-grey water. The water was pushing him up against the roof. The roof was sharp and pained his back. He pulled himself along with his hands – fast, fast – and used his legs as levers. His head knocked against something; a sharp pain dizzied him. Fifty, fifty-one, fifty-two . . . He was without light, and the water seemed to press upon him with the weight of rock. Seventy-one, seventy-two . . . There was no strain on his lungs. He felt like an inflated balloon, his lungs were so light and easy, but his head was pulsing.

He was being continually pressed against the sharp roof, which felt slimy as well as sharp. Again he thought of octopuses, and wondered if the tunnel might be filled with weed that could tangle him. He gave himself a panicky, convulsive kick forward, ducked his head, and swam. His feet and hands moved freely, as if in open water. The hole must have widened out. He thought he must be swimming fast, and he was frightened of banging his head if the tunnel narrowed.

A hundred, a hundred and one . . . The water paled. Victory filled him. His lungs were beginning to hurt. A few more strokes and he would be out. He was counting wildly; he said a hundred and fifteen, and then, a long time later, a hundred and fifteen again. The water was a clear jewel-green all around him. Then he saw, above his head, a crack running up through the rock. Sunlight was falling through it, showing the clean, dark rock of the tunnel, a single mussel shell, and darkness ahead.

He was at the end of what he could do. He looked up at the crack as if it were filled with air and not water, as if he could put his mouth to it and draw air. A hundred and fifteen, he heard himself say inside his head – but he had said that long ago. He must go on into the blackness ahead, or he would drown. His head was swelling, his lungs cracking. A hundred and fifteen, a hundred and fifteen pounded through his head, and he feebly clutched at rocks in the dark, pulling himself forward, leaving the

brief space of sunlit water behind. He felt he was dying. He was no longer quite conscious. He struggled on in the darkness between lapses into unconsciousness. An immense, swelling pain filled his head, and then the darkness cracked with an explosion of green light. His hands, groping forward, met nothing; and his feet, kicking back, propelled him out into the open sea.

He drifted to the surface, his face turned up to the air. He was gasping like a fish. He felt he would sink now and drown; he could not swim the few feet back to the rock. Then he was clutching it and pulling himself up on to it. He lay face down, gasping. He could see nothing but a red-veined, clotted dark. His eyes must have burst, he thought; they were full of blood. He tore off his goggles and a gout of blood went into the sea. His nose was bleeding, and the blood had filled the goggles.

He scooped up handfuls of water from the cool, salty sea, to splash on his face, and did not know whether it was blood or salt water he tasted. After a time, his heart quietened, his eyes cleared, and he sat up. He could see the local boys diving and playing half a mile away. He did not want them. He wanted nothing but to get back home and lie down.

In a short while, Jerry swam to the shore and climbed slowly up the path to the villa. He flung himself on his bed and slept, waking at the sound of feet on the path outside. His mother was coming back. He rushed to the bathroom, thinking she must not see his face with bloodstains, or tearstains, on it. He came out of the bathroom and met her as she walked into the villa, smiling, her eyes lighting up.

'Have a nice morning?' she asked, laying her hand on his warm brown shoulder a moment.

'Oh yes, thank you,' he said.

'You look a bit pale.' And then, sharp and anxious, 'How did you bang your head?'

'Oh, just banged it,' he told her.

She looked at him closely. He was strained; his eyes were glazed-looking. She was worried. And then she said to herself, Oh, don't fuss! Nothing can happen. He can swim like a fish.

They sat down to lunch together.

'Mummy,' he said, 'I can stay under water for two minutes – three minutes, at least.' It came bursting out of him.

'Can you, darling?' she said. 'Well, I shouldn't overdo it. I don't think you ought to swim any more today.'

She was ready for a battle of wills, but he gave in at once. It was no longer of the least importance to go to the bay.

The Angel of the Central Line
Nina Bawden

This is a true story. I tell you this because I am afraid that otherwise you won't believe it. (I find it quite hard to believe myself, which is why I am writing it down so that later on in my life, when I am old, I will be able to read it and remind myself that it really happened.)

I had quarrelled with my best friend, Tom. It was the middle of winter. He lived in Notting Hill and I lived in Islington, but at that time, which was before the collapse of the cities, most outlying settlements were connected by the London Underground Railway, or, as we called it then, the tube.

I won't say what we quarrelled about because it has nothing to do with my story. All you need to know is that we had been sitting in a café close by Notting Hill Gate tube station when he said he never wanted to see me again in his life, and I said that I hoped I would never have to see him again in the next.

All the way home in the tube train I wished I was dead. As I opened the front door I heard the phone ringing and ran to answer it, but it stopped as I got there. 'Just as well,' my dad said, coming out of the kitchen. 'I told your mother we'd go to Tesco before she got back and we're running behind.'

I skidded round Tesco like an Olympic sprinter, hurling bottles and cartons and cat food and Special Offers into Dad's trolley while he lumbered along at the speed of a very old man propped on a Zimmer frame. Dad groaned a bit, but he laughed as well, and when we got back he said he could see I had better things to do with my time than provision the household, so he would do his best to carry all the stuff in by himself.

There were three messages on the answer phone.

The first said, 'Just thought I'd ring.'

The second, 'You ought to be home by now. Oh, *all right*! I'm *sorry*. OK?'

The third message was longer. 'Look. Listen. I'm going to the café *now*. It's twenty to six. I'll wait there till seven. If you don't come, OK, I'll just know that's *it*. Right?' And the phone was slammed down.

It was just before six o'clock now. It wouldn't take more than forty minutes once I got to the station; there were plenty of trains at rush hour. I yelled at Dad in the kitchen and he yelled back I was not to be later than nine o'clock, it was a school day tomorrow, I knew the rules! And *wrap up* – the barometer was dropping like a stone.

He was right about that. It was freezing outside, ice underfoot and vicious needles of sleet slashing horizontally into my face. I kept my head down, slipping and slithering, but I managed to stay upright. Then I was in the warmth of the Underground station and crashing down the escalators to the Northern Line.

There was a train waiting. I got in, but only just: lucky I'm thin, I thought. Even so, there wasn't much room to breathe. Someone said, 'Cattle, that's all we are, load of meat for the knackers,' and several people laughed, though it didn't seem all that funny. And though I was thin, I wasn't tall enough for this squash: my nose was level with a man's stinky armpit.

Not for long, though. There were only two stops between the Angel station and Bank, which was where I had to change for the Central Line to Notting Hill Gate. Bank was a huge underground station, miles of dim, leaking tunnels and crumbling spiral stairs. (Although there were a few ancient and grubby notices saying a programme of repairs was under way, there were not many people who believed this any longer.)

I knew Bank station. I could have found my way blindfold; up and down, in and out, from the Northern to the Central Line and back again. But this evening the tunnels and stairs were more crowded – and much smellier – than usual. When I started to climb the last flight of dark, winding stairs, there were so many people thundering down them that I had to cling on to the rail at the side with both hands to avoid being knocked over and trampled to death underfoot.

I heard the voice over the Tannoy: '. . . a serious fire at Stratford. There will be no more trains on the Central Line tonight.'

I managed to look at my watch. It was twenty minutes past six. If the trains were not running, there was no other way I could get to the café at Notting Hill by seven o'clock.

I thought, *it's not true*! I went on, hauling myself up the stairs, hand over hand on the rail, fighting against the flood of people, the raging tide.

A man said, as he passed, 'Central Line's closed, don't waste your time.'

I still couldn't believe it. I said, under my breath, 'No, oh, please, no . . .'

I felt a hand under my arm. Someone said 'Do you want a train? Where do you want to go?'

'Notting Hill Gate. But the Central Line's closed.'

I looked up. Very tall, a very black suit, a very black face, a white shirt, white as a swan's wing. White, white teeth – he was smiling.

I said, 'I have to get there. My granny is dying.'

I don't know why I said that. Perhaps I thought it sounded more important than a quarrel with Tom. Or I was ashamed of the quarrel.

He said, his white smile growing broader, 'Then we'll have to get you there. Find a train.'

I said, 'There aren't any trains. There's been a fire.'

But his hand was firm under my elbow. He was taking the brunt of the downward rush of the crowd on his shoulder, shielding me with his body. Then we were through a tiled arch to the Central Line.

And an empty platform. Just me, and my rescuer, and the voice from the Tannoy. It said, echoing through the tunnels, 'There will be no more trains on the Central Line tonight.'

My rescuer said, 'It will be all right. Trust me. There will be a train very soon.'

I thought he must be mad. But he looked perfectly sane.

He said, again, 'Trust me.' And, in that very same moment, I heard the distant rattle-bang-roar of the approaching train. Then its lights flashing yellow in the dark of the tunnel, then the swish and the rumble as it drew into the station. And stopped.

The doors opened. Although I could see people on board, no one moved. When we got on, I saw why. There were several men and women in our carriage, and they were all asleep. I sat down on an empty seat and my companion sat opposite. He smiled at me and, as the train started up again, said – speaking softly, as if he didn't want to wake the other passengers, 'It is Notting Hill Gate you want, isn't it?'

I said, 'Yes,' and he nodded, as if setting this down in his memory. Then he closed his eyes and seemed to fall, like everyone else, into a deep, peaceful slumber.

The train didn't stop at St Paul's, or Chancery Lane, or Holborn, or Tottenham Court Road. It slowed down as we went through Oxford Circus, but there was no one waiting on the platform and, in the end, it didn't stop there either. The same thing – no one waiting, the train slowing but not stopping – happened at Bond Street and Marble Arch. But my friend woke up. He said, 'Notting Hill Gate?'

I said, 'Not yet. There's Lancaster Gate and Queensway first.'

I was suddenly beginning to be afraid. There must be something wrong. Perhaps this wasn't a real train but a ghost train, and all the sleeping people were dead. Perhaps they had died in the fire. Perhaps I was dead too.

But I didn't believe in ghosts.

My friend smiled his white smile. He said, 'Please do not worry.'

The train stopped at Queensway. There were two men in the uniform of London Underground on the platform. They turned as the train drew in and I thought they looked puzzled.

I said, hearing my voice rising, high and nervous, 'It's the next stop.'

'I know,' he said. His eyelids drooped and he seemed to doze. But when we arrived at Notting Hill Gate, they snapped open and his dark eyes were bright. 'You will be all right now,' he said.

The doors opened. Two of the passengers, an old man with a black and grey beard, and a boy with a gold stud in his eyebrow, woke up, yawning, looking about them, and then made a rush for the door. They stumbled on to the platform at the same time as I did but they took no notice of me, nor of each other.

The train doors closed with a hiss. And I ran.

I ran up the escalator, up the stairs. There was no one in the ticket hall. The tobacconist and stationer's was boarded up. A sign on a tripod said, 'Station Closed'.

I ran up the dirty concrete steps to the street. There was light and traffic and people. I breathed in exhaust fumes and tasted the lovely smell of real life.

It was five minutes to seven. I hopped from one foot to another until the red man turned green and went walking; then I flew over the road, a few hundred yards to the café where Tom was waiting.

*

I didn't tell him. I felt too embarrassed. (And I didn't want him to know that I had minded so much!)

I didn't tell my mother and father either. Not even when they said on the nine o'clock news (I was in at one minute to nine) that the Central Line had been closed from five-thirty this evening and there would be no more trains tonight. All I said was that I knew all about *that*! I had come home on the Circle Line to King's Cross and it had taken me ages.

But I told my grandmother. She listened and smiled and her eyes went misty. She said, 'That was an angel, of course. Either your guardian angel or the Underground angel. It's good to know they still do a bit of work for their living.'

I said, 'You don't believe that!'

'Can you think of a better explanation?'

I said, ashamed, 'I told him that you were dying.'

She laughed. 'I'm glad you think my death might be important enough to persuade an angel to get on the job so efficiently!'

I said indignantly, 'But it was a lie!'

And she laughed again. She said, 'Any angel worth his salt would know that.'

The Bewitched Jacket
Dino Buzzati

Although I appreciate elegant dress, I don't usually pay attention to the perfection (or imperfection) with which my companions' clothing is cut.

Nonetheless, one night during a reception at a house in Milan, I met a man about forty years old who literally shone because of the simple and decisive beauty of his clothes.

I don't know who he was, I was meeting him for the first time, and at the introduction, as always happens, it was impossible to get his name. But at a certain point during the evening, I found myself near him, and we began to talk. He seemed a civil, well-bred man, but with an air of sadness. Perhaps with exaggerated familiarity – God should have stopped me – I complimented him on his elegance; and I even dared to ask him who his tailor might be.

He smiled curiously, as if he had expected my question. 'Nearly no one knows him,' he said. 'Still, he's a great master. And he works only when it comes to him. For a few initiates.'

'So that I couldn't . . . ?'

'Oh, try, try. His name is Corticella, Alfonso Corticella, via Ferrara 17.'

'He will be expensive, I imagine.'

'I believe so, but I swear I don't know. He made me this suit three years ago, and he still hasn't sent me the bill.'

'Corticella? Via Ferrara 17, did you say?'

'Exactly,' the stranger answered. And he left me to join another group of people.

At via Ferrara 17, I found a house like so many others and like those of so many other tailors; it was the residence of Alfonso Corticella. It was he who came to let me in. He was a little old man with black hair, which was, however, obviously dyed.

To my surprise, he was not hard to deal with. In fact, he seemed eager for me to be his customer. I explained to him how I had got his address, praised his cutting, and asked him to make me a suit. We selected a grey wool, then he took my measurements, and offered to come to my apartment for the fitting. I asked him the price. There was no hurry, he answered, we could always come to an agreement. What a congenial man, I thought at first. Nevertheless, later, while I was returning home, I realized that the little old man had left me feeling uneasy (perhaps because of his much too warm and persistent smiles). In short, I had no desire at all to see him again. But now the suit had been ordered. And after about three weeks it was ready.

When they brought it to me, I tried it on in front of a mirror for a little while. It was a masterpiece. Yet, I don't know why, perhaps because of my memory of the unpleasant old man, I didn't have any desire to wear it. And weeks passed before I decided to do so.

That day I shall remember forever. It was a Tuesday in April and it was raining. When I had slipped into the clothes – jacket, trousers and **vest** – I was pleased to observe that they didn't pull and weren't tight anywhere, as almost always happens with new suits. And yet they wrapped me perfectly.

As a rule I put nothing in the right jacket pocket; in the left one, I keep my cards. This explains why, only after a couple of hours at the office, casually slipping my hand into the right pocket, I noticed that there was a piece of paper inside. Was it maybe the tailor's bill?

No. It was a ten thousand lire note.

vest: in the United States, a waistcoat

I was astounded. I certainly had not put it there. On the other hand, it was absurd to think it a joke of the tailor Corticella. Much less did it seem a gift from my maid, the only person, other than the tailor, who had occasion to go near my suit. Or was it a counterfeit note? I looked at it in the light, I compared it to other ones. It couldn't be any better than these.

There was a single possible explanation: Corticella's absent-mindedness. Perhaps a customer had come to make a payment. The tailor didn't have his wallet with him just then, and so to avoid leaving the money around, he slipped it into my jacket, which was hanging on a mannequin. These things can happen.

I rang for my secretary. I wanted to write a letter to Corticella, returning the money that was not mine. Yet (and I can't say why I did it) I slipped my hand into the pocket again.

'Is anything wrong, sir? Do you feel ill?' asked my secretary, who entered at that moment. I must have turned pale as death. In my pocket my fingers touched the edge of another strip of paper – which had not been there a few minutes before.

'No, no, it's nothing,' I said. 'A slight dizziness. It happens to me sometimes. Maybe I'm a little tired. You can go now, dear, I wanted to dictate a letter, but we'll do it later.'

Only after my secretary had gone did I dare remove the piece of paper from my pocket. It was another ten thousand lire note. Then I tried a third time. And a third banknote came out.

My heart began to race. I had the feeling for some mysterious reason I was involved in the plot of a fairytale, like those that are told to children and that no one believes are true.

On the pretext that I was not feeling well, I left the office and went home. I needed to be alone. Luckily, my maid had already gone. I shut the doors, lowered the blinds. I began to take out the notes one after another, very quickly. My pocket seemed inexhaustible.

I worked in a spasmodic nervous tension, with the fear that the miracle might stop at any moment. I wanted it to continue all day and night, until I had accumulated billions. But at a certain point the flow diminished.

Before me stood an impressive heap of banknotes. The important thing now was to hide them, so no one might get wind of the affair. I emptied an old trunk full of rugs and put the money, arranged in many little piles, at the bottom. Then I slowly began counting. There were 58 million lire.

I awoke the next morning after the maid arrived. She was amazed to find me in bed still completely dressed. I tried to laugh, explaining that I had drunk a little too much the night before and sleep had suddenly seized me.

A new anxiety arose: she asked me to take off the suit, so she could at least give it a brushing.

I answered that I had to go out immediately and didn't have time to change. Then I hurried to a store selling ready-to-wear clothes to buy another suit made of similar material; I would leave this one in the maid's care; 'mine', the suit that in the course of a few days would make me one of the most powerful men in the world, I would hide in a safe place.

I didn't know whether I was living in a dream, whether I was happy or rather suffocating under the burden of too hard a fate. On the street, I was continually feeling the magic pocket through my raincoat. Each time I breathed a sigh of relief. Beneath the cloth answered the comforting crackle of paper money.

But a single coincidence cooled my joyous delirium. News of a robbery that occurred the day before headlined the morning papers. A bank's armoured car, after making the rounds of the branches, was carrying the day's deposits to the main office when it was seized and cleaned out in viale Palmanova by four criminals. As people swarmed around the scene, one of the gangsters began to shoot to keep them away. A passerby was killed. But, above all, the amount of the loot struck me: it was exactly 58 million – like the money I had put in the trunk.

Could there be a connection between my sudden wealth and the criminal raid that happened almost simultaneously? It seemed foolish to think so. What's more, I am not superstitious. All the same, the incident left me very confused.

The more one gets, the more one wants. I was already rich, considering my modest habits. But the illusion of a life of unlimited luxury was compelling. And that same evening I set to work again. Now I proceeded more slowly, with less torture to my nerves. Another 135 million was added to my previous treasure.

That night I couldn't close my eyes. Was it the presentiment of danger? Or the tormented conscience of one who undeservedly wins a fabulous fortune? Or was it a kind of confused remorse? At dawn I leaped from the bed, dressed, and ran outside to get a newspaper.

As I read, I lost my breath. A terrible fire, which had begun in a **naphtha** warehouse, had half-destroyed a building on the main street, via San Cloro. The flames had consumed, among other things, the safes of a large real estate company which contained more than 130 million in cash. Two firemen met their deaths in the blaze.

Should I now, perhaps, list my crimes one by one? Yes, because now I knew that the money the jacket gave me came from those crimes, from blood, from desperation and death, from hell. But I was still within the snare of reason, which scornfully refused to admit that I was in

---

naphtha: inflammable oil, such as petroleum

any way responsible. And the temptation resumed, then the hand – it was so easy! slipped into the pocket, and the fingers, with the quickest delight, grasped the edges of always another banknote. The money, the divine money!

Without moving out of my old apartment (so as not to attract attention), I soon bought a huge villa, owned a precious collection of paintings, drove around in luxurious automobiles, and having left my firm for 'reasons of health', travelled back and forth throughout the world in the company of marvellous women.

I knew that whenever I drew money from the jacket, something base and painful happened in the world. But it was still always a vague awareness, not supported by logical proofs. Meanwhile, at each new collection, my conscience was degraded, becoming more and more vile. And the tailor? I telephoned him to ask for the bill, but no one answered. In via Ferrara, when I went to search for him, they told me that he had emigrated abroad, they didn't know where. Everything then conspired to show me that without knowing it, I was bound in a pact with the Devil.

Until one morning, in the building where I lived for many years, they found a sixty-year-old retired woman asphyxiated by gas; she had killed herself for having mislaid her monthly pension of 30 thousand lire, which she had collected the day before (and which had ended up in my hands).

Enough, enough! In order not to sink to the depths of the abyss, I had to rid myself of the jacket. And not by surrendering it to someone else, because the horror would continue (who would ever be able to resist such enticement?). Its destruction was absolutely necessary.

By car I arrived at a secluded valley in the Alps. I left the car in a grassy clearing and set out in the direction of the forest. There wasn't a living soul in sight. Having gone beyond the forest, I reached the rocky ground of the moraine. Here, between two gigantic boulders, I pulled the wicked jacket from the knapsack, sprinkled it with kerosene, and lit it. In a few minutes only ashes were left.

But at the last flicker of the flames, behind me – it seemed about two or three metres away – a human voice resounded: 'Too late, too late!' Terrified, I turned around with a serpent's snap. But I saw no one. I explored the area, jumping from one huge rock to another, to hunt out the damned person. Nothing. There were only rocks.

Notwithstanding the fright I experienced, I went back down to the base of the valley with a feeling of relief. I was free at last. And rich, luckily.

But my car was no longer in the grassy clearing. And after I returned to the city, my sumptuous villa had disappeared; in its place was an uncultivated field with some poles that bore the notice 'Municipal Land For Sale'. My savings accounts were also completely drained, but I couldn't explain how. The big packets of deeds in my numerous safe-deposit boxes had vanished too. And there was dust, nothing but dust, in the old trunk.

Now I resumed working with difficulty, I hardly get through a day, and what is stranger, no one seems to be amazed by my sudden ruin.

And I know that it's still not over, I know that one day my doorbell will ring. I'll answer it and find that cursed tailor before me, with his contemptible smile, asking for the final settling of my account.

The Secret Life of Walter Mitty
James Thurber

'We're going through!' The Commander's voice was like thin ice breaking. He wore his full-dress uniform, with the heavily braided white cap pulled down rakishly over one cold grey eye. 'We can't make it, sir. It's spoiling for a hurricane, if you ask me.' 'I'm not asking you, Lieutenant Berg,' said the Commander. 'Throw on the power lights!' Rev her up to 8,500! We're going through!' The pounding of the cylinders increased: ta-pocketa-pocketa-pocketa-*pocketa-pocketa*. The Commander stared at the ice forming on the pilot window. He walked over and twisted a row of complicated dials. 'Switch on No. 8 auxiliary!' he shouted. 'Switch on No. 8 auxiliary!' repeated Lieutenant Berg. 'Full strength in No. 3 turret!' shouted the Commander. 'Full strength in No. 3 turret!' The crew, bending to their various tasks in the huge, hurtling eight-engined Navy hydroplane, looked at each other and grinned. 'The Old Man'll get us through,' they said to one another. 'The Old Man ain't afraid of Hell!' . . .

'Not so fast! You're driving too fast!' said Mrs Mitty. 'What are you driving so fast for?'

'Hmmm?' said Walter Mitty. He looked at his wife, in the seat beside him, with shocked astonishment. She seemed grossly unfamiliar, like a strange woman who had yelled at him in a crowd. 'You were up to fifty-five,' she said. 'You know I don't like to go more than forty. You were up to fifty-five.' Walter Mitty drove on through Waterbury in silence, the roaring of the SN202 through the worst storm in twenty years of Navy flying fading in the remote, intimate airways of his mind. 'You're tensed up again,' said Mrs Mitty. 'It's one of your days. I wish you'd let Dr Renshaw look you over.'

Walter Mitty stopped the car in front of the building where his wife went to have her hair done. 'Remember to get those overshoes while I'm having my hair done,' she said. 'I don't need overshoes,' said Mitty. She put her mirror back in her bag. 'We've been through all that,' she said, getting out of the car. 'You're not a young man any longer.' He raced the engine a little. 'Why don't you wear your gloves? Have you lost your gloves?' Walter Mitty reached in a pocket and brought out the gloves. He put them on, but after she had turned and gone into the building and he had driven on to a red light, he took them off again. 'Pick it up, brother!' snapped a cop as the light changed, and Mitty hastily pulled on his gloves and lurched ahead. He drove around the streets aimlessly for a time, and then he drove past the hospital on his way to the parking lot.

. . . 'It's the millionaire banker, Wellington McMillan,' said the pretty nurse. 'Yes?' said Walter Mitty, removing his gloves slowly. 'Who has the case?' 'Dr Renshaw and Dr Benbow, but there are two specialists here, Dr Remington from New York and Mr Pritchard-Mitford from London. He flew over.' A door opened down a long, cool corridor and Dr Renshaw came out. He looked distraught and haggard. 'Hello, Mitty,' he said. 'We're having the devil's own time with McMillan, the millionaire banker and close personal friend of **Roosevelt**. Obstreosis of the ductal tract. Tertiary. Wish you'd take a look at him.' 'Glad to,' said Mitty.

In the operating room there were whispered introductions: 'Dr Remington, Dr Mitty. Mr Pritchard-Mitford, Dr Mitty.' 'I've read your book on streptothricosis,' said Pritchard-Mitford, shaking hands. 'A brilliant performance, sir.' 'Thank you,' said Walter Mitty. 'Didn't know you were in the States, Mitty,' grumbled

---

Roosevelt: an American President

Remington. 'Coals to Newcastle, bringing Mitford and me up here for a tertiary.' 'You are very kind,' said Mitty. A huge, complicated machine, connected to the operating table, with many tubes and wires, began at this moment to go pocketa-pocketa-pocketa. 'The new anaesthetizer is giving way!' shouted an interne. 'There is no one in the East who knows how to fix it!' 'Quiet, man!' said Mitty, in a low, cool voice. He sprang to the machine, which was now going pocketa-pocketa-queep-pocketa-queep. He began fingering delicately a row of glistening dials. 'Give me a fountain pen!' he snapped. Someone handed him a fountain pen. He pulled a faulty piston out of the machine and inserted the pen in its place. 'That will hold it for ten minutes,' he said. 'Get on with the operation.' A nurse hurried over and whispered to Renshaw, and Mitty saw the man turn pale. 'Coreopsis has set in,' said Renshaw nervously. 'If you would take over, Mitty?' Mitty looked at him and at the **craven** figure of Benbow, who drank, and at the grave, uncertain faces of the two great specialists. 'If you wish,' he said. They slipped a white gown on him; he adjusted a mask and drew on thin gloves; nurses handed him shining . . .

'Back it up, Mac! Look out for that Buick!' Walter Mitty jammed on the brakes. 'Wrong lane, Mac,' said the parking-lot attendant, looking at Mitty closely. 'Gee. Yeh,' muttered Mitty. He began cautiously to back out of the lane marked 'Exit Only'. 'Leave her sit there,' said the attendant. 'I'll put her away.' Mitty got out of the car. 'Hey, better leave the key.' 'Oh,' said Mitty, handing the man the ignition key. The attendant vaulted into the car, backed it up with insolent skill, and put it where it belonged.

They're so damn cocky, thought Walter Mitty, walking along Main Street; they think they know everything. Once he had tried to take his **chains** off, outside New Milford,

---

craven: cowardly

chains: used to give tyres grip in snow

and he had got them wound around the axles. A man had had to come out in a wrecking car and unwind them, a young, grinning garageman. Since then Mrs Mitty always made him drive to a garage to have the chains taken off. The next time, he thought, I'll wear my right arm in a sling; they won't grin at me then. I'll have my right arm in a sling and they'll see I couldn't possibly take the chains off myself. He kicked at the slush on the sidewalk. 'Overshoes,' he said to himself, and he began looking for a shoe store.

When he came out into the street again, with the overshoes in a box under his arm, Walter Mitty began to wonder what the other thing was his wife had told him to get. She had told him twice, before they set out from their house in Waterbury. In a way he hated these weekly trips to town – he was always getting something wrong. Kleenex, he thought, Squibb's, razor blades? No. Toothpaste, toothbrush, bicarbonate, carborundum, initiative and referendum? He gave it up. But she would remember it. 'Where's the what's-its-name?' she would ask. 'Don't tell me you forgot the what's-its-name.' A news-boy went by shouting something about the Waterbury trial.

. . . 'Perhaps this will refresh your memory.' The District Attorney suddenly thrust a heavy automatic at the quiet figure on the witness stand. 'Have you ever seen this before?' Walter Mitty took the gun and examined it expertly. 'This is my Webley-Vickers 50.80,' he said calmly. An excited buzz ran round the courtroom. The judge rapped for order. 'You are a crack shot with any sort of firearms, I believe?' said the District Attorney, insinuatingly. 'Objection!' shouted Mitty's attorney. 'We have shown that the defendant could not have fired the shot. We have shown that he wore his right arm in a sling on the night of the fourteenth of July.' Walter Mitty raised his hand briefly and the bickering attorneys were stilled. 'With any known make of gun,' he said evenly, 'I could have killed Gregory Fitzhurst at three hundred feet *with my left hand*.' Pandemonium broke loose in the courtroom. A woman's scream rose above the bedlam and suddenly a lovely, dark-haired girl was in Walter Mitty's arms. The District Attorney struck at her savagely. Without rising from his chair, Mitty let the man have it on the point of the chin. 'You miserable *cur*!' . . .

'Puppy biscuit,' said Walter Mitty. He stopped walking and the buildings of Waterbury rose up out of the misty courtroom and surrounded him again. A woman who was passing laughed. 'He said "puppy biscuit",' she said to her companion. 'That man said "puppy biscuit" to himself.' Walter Mitty hurried on. He went into an A and P, not the first one he came to but a smaller one farther up the street. 'I want some biscuit for small, young dogs,' he said to the clerk. 'Any special brand, sir?' The greatest pistol shot in the world thought for a moment. 'It says "Puppies bark for It" on the box,' said Walter Mitty.

His wife would be through at the hairdressers in fifteen minutes, Mitty saw in looking at his watch, unless they had trouble drying it; sometimes they had trouble drying it. She didn't like to get to the hotel first; she would want him to be there waiting for her as usual. He found a big leather chair in the lobby, facing a window, and he put the overshoes and the puppy biscuit on the floor beside it. He picked up an old copy of *Liberty* and sank down into the chair. 'Can Germany Conquer the World Through the Air?' Walter Mitty looked at the pictures of bombing planes and of ruined streets.

. . . 'The **cannonading** has got the wind up in young Raleigh, sir,' said the sergeant. Captain Mitty looked up at him through tousled hair. 'Get him to bed,' he said

---

cur: dog
cannonading: sound of gunfire

wearily. 'With the others. I'll fly alone.' 'But you can't, sir,' said the sergeant anxiously. 'It takes two men to handle that bomber and the Archies are pounding hell out of the air. Von Richtman's circus is between here and Saulier.' 'Somebody's got to get that ammunition dump,' said Mitty. 'I'm going over. Spot of brandy?' He poured a drink for the sergeant and one for himself. War thundered and whined around the dugout and battered at the door. There was a rending of wood and splinters flew through the room. 'A bit of a near thing,' said Captain Mitty carelessly. 'The box barrage is closing in,' said the sergeant. 'We only live once, Sergeant,' said Mitty, with his faint, fleeting smile. 'Or do we?' He poured another brandy and tossed it off. 'I never see a man could hold his brandy like you, sir,' said the sergeant. 'Begging your pardon, sir.' Captain Mitty stood up and strapped on his huge Webley-Vickers automatic. 'It's forty kilometres through hell, sir,' said the sergeant. Mitty finished one last brandy. 'After all', he said softly, 'what isn't?' The pounding of the cannon increased; there was the rat-tat-tatting of machine-guns, and from somewhere came the menacing pocketa-pocketa-pocketa of the new flame-throwers. Walter Mitty walked to the door of the dugout humming 'Auprès de ma Blonde'. He turned and waved to the sergeant. 'Cheerio!' he said . . .

Something struck his shoulder. 'I've been looking all over this hotel for you,' said Mrs Mitty. 'Why did you have to hide in this old chair? How did you expect me to find you?' 'Things close in,' said Walter Mitty vaguely. 'What?' Mrs Mitty said. 'Did you get the what's-its-name? The puppy biscuit. What's in that box?' 'Overshoes,' said Mitty. 'Couldn't you have put them on in the store?' 'I was thinking,' said Walter Mitty. 'Doesn't it ever occur to you that sometimes I am thinking?' She looked at him. 'I'm going to take your temperature when I get you home,' she said.

They went out through the revolving doors that made

a faintly derisive whistling sound when you pushed them. It was two blocks to the parking lot. At the drugstore on the corner she said, 'Wait here for me. I forgot something, I won't be a minute.' She was more than a minute. Walter Mitty lighted a cigarette. It began to rain, rain with sleet in it. He stood up against the wall of the drugstore, smoking. . . . He put his shoulders back and his heels together. 'To hell with the handkerchief,' said Walter Mitty scornfully. He took one last drag on his cigarette and snapped it away. Then, with that faint, fleeting smile playing about his lips, he faced the firing squad; erect and motionless, proud and disdainful, Walter Mitty the Undefeated, **inscrutable** to the last.

---

inscrutable: impossible to know fully

Activities

Starters

Momster in the Closet **by Jane Yolen**
Incident at Dusk **by Claudia Baharini**

1 Both these stories tease you by:

- creating a surprise ending from an unexpected *viewpoint*

- dropping false clues about what *kind* of story you're reading.

a) As a class, talk about how each writer tries to keep you guessing about what's going on. Do they succeed?

b) In pairs, take one story each. Re-read it. Then draw up a grid to show what clues there are that point ahead to the ending. Do it like this:

Momster in the Closet	
Clue	**How it fits in with the ending**
'"Grumpf ouff," Dad said, his mouth full'	Dad, who's a vampire, is gulping down human blood for his meal
'I bared my fangs at him'	Kenny's sister, also a vampire, naturally calls her teeth 'fangs'

Incident at Dusk	
Clue	**How it fits in with the ending**
'Gub' spelled backwards is 'Bug'	the narrator, a friend of Gub's, is a tiny insect
'The object was circular . . . looking like a gigantic saucer'	the 'object' is really a fruit plate but from the narrator's viewpoint it will look gigantic

Try to find up to *five* clues. Then explain them to each other. Can you find any that your partner has missed?

2 *Incident at Dusk* turns out to have a very ordinary *setting*: someone's kitchen. However, as you read it the setting seems quite different.

    a) **In small groups,** find evidence that the setting at various points suggests:

- a War Story
- a Science Fiction Story
- a Horror Story
- a 'Disaster' Story.

Are there any more types of story, or 'genres', which you are reminded of as you read?

    b) **As a class,** compare your findings. Quote phrases and sentences from the stories to back up your ideas.

Then, with your teacher's help, draw up a list of at least *six* story genres. Opposite each one note down a typical setting for it, or a setting which you connect with it from your previous reading. Display your finished list as a class poster.

3 **By yourself,** re-write either *Momster in the Closet* or *Incident at Dusk* from a different viewpoint.

You could, for example, write the former from the point of view of Kenny – or you could write the latter from the point of view of the human being.

Whichever choice you make, limit your writing to 200–250 words. Write in the first person, i.e. as if you are one of the people in the story. Try hard to get inside the character's mind and to work out before you begin:

- what they will be thinking and feeling in the story
- how they will 'see' things in a different way
- the language they will use to tell the story.

Relationships

Thank You, M'am by Langston Hughes

The Examination Result by Alun Williams

1 *Thank You, M'am* has only two characters. The story is based on the relationship between them.

a) **By yourself,** write a 5–6 line description of Mrs Luella Bates Washington Jones. Include your impressions of:

- her appearance
- the way she speaks
- her everyday life
- what her actions show about her
- what you can tell about her character from the way she treats Roger.

b) **As a class,** compare your ideas about Mrs Jones. Listen carefully to what other people say. Add to your own description any new points you agree with.

c) **By yourself,** make a character grid about Mrs Jones by **i)** listing her main character points and **ii)** adding for *each* of these a brief quotation from the story to illustrate it. Set your grid out like this:

Character point	Quotation to show this
1 a strong, forceful personality who won't let people get the better of her	'Then she reached down, picked the boy up by his shirt front, and shook him until his teeth rattled'
2	

2 Put yourself in the place of Roger, the boy in *Thank You, M'am.*

a) **In pairs,** look closely at **i)** what he *says* to Mrs Jones at different points in the story and **ii)** how the things he says show his *feelings* towards her as the story goes on.

b) **As a class,** talk about how Roger's feelings change between the beginning and the end of the story. *Why* do they change?

c) **In small groups,** pretend you have been employed to turn this story into a very short play for radio. The *dialogue* – i.e. conversation – lasts only 3 minutes.

Roger speaks fourteen times in the story. Choose the *five* occasions which you agree are the most important in showing his changing feelings towards Mrs Jones. Write out Roger's words on a large sheet of paper with a space between each speech.

Now take turns to fill each space with instructions for the actor playing Roger about the tone of voice in which to speak the five lines you've chosen. Practise saying them aloud in your group before you decide what to write.

3 In *The Examination Result* the central relationship is that between Alun (the narrator) and Cornelius.

In small groups, put Cornelius in the Hot Seat. One person plays the part of Cornelius and acts in character. Everyone else questions him about his reasons for treating Alun in the way he does.

The interviewers should first draw up a list of *at least five* questions to put to Cornelius. For example:

Why was it so important to you that Alun passed his exam?

Why did you hit Alun with such violence?

. and so on.

Before you start the Hot Seat session, let the person who is playing Cornelius see the questions and look back at the story, so that they can prepare answers to the questions.

Your Hot Seat session should take between 5 and 10 minutes. If possible, tape-record it so that later on you can compare your work with that of other groups.

4 The story of *The Examination Result* is told in the first person and the viewpoint throughout is that of Alun himself.

   As a class, discuss why the writer might have chosen to tell the story in this way. Would it have made any difference if we had seen the events through Cornelius' eyes? Does having Alun as the narrator encourage us to feel *sympathy* for him?

5 **As a class,** hold a brief discussion about what's meant by 'writing in role'. Recall any occasions when you have done this before.

   By yourself, do one of these pieces of role-writing:

   a) Put yourself in the place of Mrs Jones in *Thank You, M'am.* Describe your meeting with Roger, either in your personal diary or in a telephone call to a friend. Bring out your feelings towards him at different points in the story.

   b) Put yourself in the place of Cornelius in *The Examination Result.* Write a private letter to Alun after the story ends, but when you are still feeling angry. Bring out your feelings about how you behaved towards him at different points in the story.

Why did you depend on Alun so much + none of the other ones? He was the youngest and he was going to be the following footsteps and Cornileus was kind of the father figure to Alun too he was the the youngest.

Crimes

Shatter Proof **by Jack Ritchie**

The Sweet Old Lady Who Cried Wolf **by Mari Waagaard**

1 *Shatter Proof* is a Crime Story in which no crime is committed.

   As a class, discuss how the writer manages to hold your interest as you read.

   Go on to discuss whether stories *have* to contain a lot of 'action' in order to be effective. Refer to your previous reading as you talk about this.

2 In *Shatter Proof* the 'balance of power' between Mr Williams and the hired killer Mr Smith changes as the story goes on.

   a) **In pairs,** look back over the story. Find the key points where **i)** Mr Williams' position becomes gradually stronger and **ii)** Mr Smith's position becomes gradually weaker. Note them down like this:

Steps in the story ➜	How they change the balance of power
1 Mr Smith accepts the offer of a drink ➜	gives Mr Williams time to work out how to stay alive and how to deal with the killer
2	

   b) When you have finished, **join up with another pair.** Compare your notes. Have you chosen the same points in the story? Discuss why, or why not.

3 Imagine that this story is the first part of a TV film. The second, and final, part will show Mr Smith at the Petersons' house on the same night. He has gone there intending to kill Mrs Williams.

   a) **As a class,** talk about several *different* ways the story could develop at this point. Be ingenious – but make your ideas believable as well as dramatic.

   b) **By yourself,** decide which scene at the Petersons' will make the best ending for *Shatter Proof: the TV version.* Then write this scene in the form of a script for television. You will obviously have to create dialogue. You can also add instructions for the TV producer about the setting, sound effects, different camera shots, etc.

4 *The Sweet Old Lady Who Cried Wolf* is meant to keep the reader guessing.

   a) **In pairs**, test out how well the writer creates a feeling of *suspense* by recalling your reactions to the story when you first read it. Say:

   • what you thought of Mrs Werle in the opening section, when she visited the police station

   • what you thought would happen after the students' conversation on page 26.

   • what you thought Mrs Werle's reasons were for using the hidden tape recorder

   • what you thought was likely to happen when Mrs Werle took Jorgen and Ellida to the 'secret room'

   • what you thought would happen when Mrs Werle returned to the police station at the end.

   b) **By yourself**, write briefly about Mari Waagaard's use of suspense in this story. Say whether you think it adds to the story's interest – and in what way.

5 *The Sweet Old Lady Who Cried Wolf* is about a murderer, Mrs Werle, who gets away with it.

   a) **In small groups**, note down as many reasons as you can find to explain *why* Mrs Werle succeeds. Fill in a copy of the grid below as you talk.

Mrs Werle's 'perfect murder'			
Her character and background	How she outwits Jorgen and Ellida	How she fools the police	Other factors

   b) **As a class**, compare your findings.

   What clues does the story give about Mrs Werle's *motives* for murder? Do you think she has killed before?

6 In *The Sweet Old Lady Who Cried Wolf*, the narrative viewpoint keeps changing.

   As a class, find places in the story where we see **i)** the events and **ii)** the main character from the viewpoint of:

   • Chief Constable Ole Gregersen

   • Jorgen and Ellida

   • Mrs Werle herself.

   What do you think the writer gains by showing Mrs Werle from several viewpoints as the story unfolds? Does it make the plot harder to follow – or does it add to the story's appeal?

Ghosts

Woman and Home **by Robert Westall**
Farthing House **by Susan Hill**

1 'The house caught him'

In *Woman and Home* Miss Marriner's spirit gradually draws Higginson towards her. They 'meet' on page 48 when he comes face to face with her portrait.

a) In small groups, imagine you are making a film of this story. Select *five* key points in the plot where your film will show Miss Marriner guiding the boy to meet her. Make a plot chart to 'track' this, either in the form of a flow diagram or in some other way, such as:

What happens to Higginson	How Miss Marriner is controlling him
1 he plays truant and has to find somewhere to hide: he knows his Head of Year will be searching for him (p.36)	she has made her house seem 'inviting' as a place to hide – he is 'utterly lost' – the gate is standing half-open so he goes into the drive
2	

Add notes about how, at each point you choose, your film will show Miss Marriner's hold on Higginson becoming stronger.

b) As a class, compare **i)** your completed diagrams/charts and **ii)** the notes you have made. See if you can agree on which 'key points' in the plot *must* be highlighted in the film.

2 All Ghost Stories build up a strong *atmosphere* – often one of mystery, fear, menace, etc.

a) **In small groups**, talk about what kinds of atmosphere are created by these descriptions from *Woman and Home*:

- 'Lumps of the wistaria had grown out uncontrolled . . . They swayed crazily, dangerously.' (page 38)
- 'Immediately the clock began to tick . . . Then suddenly, without warning, it chimed. Loud and strong, it struck ten, though the hands pointed to half past two.' (page 40)
- It lay there, still. *Too* still. Its belly wasn't going up and down. It wasn't *breathing*.' (page 43)
- 'A big American rocker with a green upholstered back and seat . . . As he passed it, he must have caught it with his sleeve. For when he glanced back from the doorway, it was rocking, rocking.' (page 44)

How could you use these moments to good effect in your film version?

b) **As a class**, find several other descriptions which create a supernatural mood and atmosphere for the story. In each case discuss **i)** what their precise *purpose* is at the point where they occur and **ii)** whether you feel they are used effectively by the writer.

3 In *Farthing House*, the story begins in the present: 'I <u>have</u> <u>never told</u> you any of this before'. It also ends in the present: 'But <u>I imagine</u> that she <u>has gone</u> . . .'

Everything in between is told in *retrospect*, i.e. looking back in time: 'I <u>was going</u> to see Aunt Addy'.

As a class, discuss why the writer might have chosen to construct the story in this way. You might consider:

- Who is the unseen character the narrator is writing for?
- Does the unseen character have anything in common with the ghost?
- How does the story's structure allow the writer to add a twist at the end?

- Do you find the final twist effective? Why, or why not?

4 As well as being Ghost Stories, these two narratives have several other features in common. They also differ in some important ways.

   a) **In pairs**, make an enlarged copy of the grid below. Use it to discuss the similarities and differences between the stories. Fill in the columns as you talk.

Features of the story	Woman and Home	Farthing House
Who is the ghost?		
Who is the ghost haunting?		
What is the ghost's *purpose* in haunting people?		
How does the main character react to being haunted?		
Does the story make you feel frightened? Why, or why not?		

* h t w

   b) **By yourself**, use your notes to plan a written comparison between *Woman and Home* and *Farthing House*. Its title will be:

   'What do these two Ghost Stories have in common, and in what ways do they differ? Which is the more effective – and why?'

   Base your plan on the grid above. Show the plan to your teacher and listen to their advice for change or

P. T.O

improvement. Then write up your comparison in essay form, using quotations to back up your ideas.

5 **By yourself**, or **in pairs**, write your own Ghost Story, based on the plot of one of these narratives.

If you choose *Woman and Home*, re-read Miss Marriner's 'Last Will and Testament' (page 50). Tell the story of one of 'the others who came' to her house. Write it in the first person ('I' . . . 'my' . . . 'we'). Try to build up a strong atmosphere of fear and the supernatural.

If you choose *Farthing House*, tell the story of someone else who was haunted by the young mother in either Farthing House or the graveyard. Use the third person ('she' . . . 'her' . . . 'it'). Try to build up a strong degree of tension and suspense – and include a twist at the end.

Your story should be 2–3 pages long.

Contrasts

My Oedipus Complex **by Frank O'Connor**

Getting Away From It All **by Ann Walsh**

1 As a class, read *My Oedipus Complex*.

a) **In small groups**, talk about the different stages of the story. How can you tell that the writer has planned out the plot in *episodes*? Discuss the points at which one episode ends and a new one begins.

b) **In pairs**, look closely at the text and make a brief summary in note form of the events in each main episode. Use the following headings to organize your discussion:

- 'The war was the most peaceful period of my life'

- 'Don't wake Daddy!'

- 'Father and I were enemies, open and avowed'

- 'Don't-wake-Sonny!'

c) **As a class**, use your notes to discuss the writer's different *purposes* in the four episodes above. How does each one mark a new development in the story?

2 Imagine you are in charge of adapting *Getting Away From It All* into a play for television.

a) **In small groups**, work out how many main episodes there are in the story. Decide which of these you need to convert into separate scenes for the TV version – and how many scenes there will be. Make a plot chart to show this like the one on the next page.

Episode in story	➡	TV scenes
1 the woman and her daughters arrive at the cabin	➡	**1a** the woman tries to make the cabin fit to live in
	➡	**1b** next morning the woman finds all the groceries have been 'savaged' by rats
2		

b) **In the same group**, work on adapting the story's final episode for TV, where the two girls meet the American tourists. Begin at 'The tourists were American, elderly, and kind,' on page 90.

Make production notes for this scene. You need to cover:

- the number and sequence of 'shots' you will show

- how you will make the scene visually interesting

- the use you will make of the story's setting at this point

- how you will establish the atmosphere of the scene

- the use you will make of sound effects (include music if you wish)

- the narrative viewpoint from which the scene will be filmed.

c) **As a class**, compare the production notes you made in your groups. Be constructively critical of each other's ideas.

3 a) **In small groups**, plan and perform an improvisation based on the passage in *My Oedipus Complex* beginning 'In the afternoon, at Mother's request,

Father took me out for a walk' and ending 'I had never met anyone so absorbed in himself as he seemed' (page 74).

The main characters are Larry and Father. Introduce some other characters who Father meets during their walk in town.

Your main purpose is to bring out the relationship between Larry and Father at this point in the story, as Larry sees it. Exactly how you do that is for you to decide.

b) **As a class**, watch several of the improvisations. Compare them with the feeling and atmosphere of the written passage they are based on. Which features of the passage have the improvisations highlighted? How effectively have they done so?

4 *My Oedipus Complex* and *Getting Away From It All* are different *types* of story. The former is a humorous piece of writing about relationships within a family. The latter is a Horror Story.

As a class, talk about how each writer uses the opening of their story to attract and hold the reader's interest. Focus on the first four paragraphs of *My Oedipus Complex*, up to 'The Geneys' baby would have done us fine' (page 72). In *Getting Away From It All*, focus on the opening section as far as 'fresh black droppings lay over everything like a satanic snowfall' (page 86).

Discuss:

- which narrative viewpoint each writer uses, and why

- what immediate impressions are given of the characters

- what hints there are about the way each story will develop

- what clues there are about the *genre* of each story.

Then give your opinion about the *effectiveness* of each opening. Which one succeeds the more in making you want to read on? Why?

5 **By yourself**, choose one of the following genres:

- a Horror Story   • a Romance   • a Murder Mystery
- an Aliens Story   • a Thriller   • a Historical Story

a) Work out the plot of a story in your mind, or make brief notes. Then plan and write the opening section of your story. Use the writing techniques you have been looking at above to establish plot, character, setting, atmosphere and narrative viewpoint.

b) Add a *plan* for the rest of the story to your opening, and then hand them in. Take your teacher's advice about both. Finally, write up your story in full, trying hard to hold the reader's interest from start to finish.

Science Fictions

Star Light by Isaac Asimov

Reunion by Arthur C Clarke

1 The plot of *Star Light* is quite hard to follow on a first reading.

  a) **In small groups**, find answers to the questions below by checking the details of the story.

- 'Old Brennmeyer had planned the whole thing'. *What* had he planned?

- Why did he need Trent to help him?

- Why did Trent have to kill Brennmeyer?

- Where is Trent escaping to? Why is he confident he can make it?

- If Trent's plans had worked out, why would he have become extremely rich?

- Why do Trent's plans collapse when he encounters the nova?

- At the end of the story, why does Trent wish he'd kept the knife he used earlier to kill Brennmeyer?

  b) **As a class**, compare the answers you've come up with in your groups. By the end of this discussion, make sure you have a clear understanding of *what* happens in the story, and *why*.

2 *Star Light* is a classic Science Fiction ('Sci-Fi') Story.

  a) **In pairs**, talk about the features of the story that make it typical of the Sci-Fi genre. Make an enlarged version of the grid overleaf to help you: fill it in as you talk.

Typical features of a Sci-Fi Story			
Events	Characters	Settings	The writer's style and language

b) Then **join up with another pair**. Compare what you have written. If you know a number of other Sci-Fi stories (or films), compare *Star Light* with some of them. Does it have any features which make it an unusual example of its genre?

c) **By yourself**, re-write an episode from *Star Light* in the style of either a typical Murder Story or a typical Horror Story. (If necessary, look back to the examples of these genres in this book.)

If you choose to write in the style of a Murder Story, you could use the episode where Trent stabs Brennmeyer to death. If you choose Horror, you could add an episode to the end of the story describing the way Trent dies.

The length of your writing is less important than the way you imitate the style and language of the genre you select.

3 The time-scale – or 'chronology' – of *Star Light* is unusual. This is because the writer weaves into his narrative, which takes place mainly in the present, snapshots from the past. In other words, there is no straightforward **A → B → C** time sequence in this narrative.

As a class, discuss the way Isaac Asimov builds up his story by mixing episodes from past and present. It begins in the present. You should be able to find *two* major 'flash-back' sections as it goes on.

Activities

Why do you think Asimov has chosen to shape the story
in this way? Is it needlessly complicated – or does it help
to catch and hold the reader's interest?

4 *Reunion* is a highly compressed and unusual story. To
understand it fully, you need to read 'between the lines'
and compare your responses with other people's.

In small groups, use the prompts below as a basis for
sharing ideas about the story.

- Who is the speaker? Who is he speaking to? What
means is he using to do so?

- What do you learn about the *history* of the speaker
and his people?

- According to the speaker, what happened on Earth
'two million years ago'?

- What message is the speaker bringing to the people
on Earth?

Take it in turns to talk about any further reactions you
have to *Reunion* – in particular, what you make of the fact
that the whole story is written from a first person
viewpoint, and that in a strict sense it has no plot.

5 Both *Star Light* and *Reunion* are Science Fiction stories. As
such, they don't describe events that could really happen
(as far as most people are concerned, that is).

As a class, discuss whether these stories do more than
simply *entertain* you or provide a brief escape from real
life. To help your discussion:

- Consider this comment on *Star Light* by an editor of
Sci-Fi Stories:

  '*As Asimov never tires of telling us, it is human
  beings and not machines that cause tragedy and
  destruction.*'

- Say how you react to the last line of *Reunion*.

Childhoods

The Doll's House **by Katherine Mansfield**

Through the Tunnel **by Doris Lessing**

1 In *The Doll's House* the Kelveys are looked down on by the other girls and their families.

   a) **In pairs**, find examples from the story of how the Kelveys are treated as 'outsiders'. Make notes of what you come up with, like this:

Reactions of other characters to the Kelveys	How these reactions make you feel as you read
'They walked past the Kelveys with their heads in the air' (p.103) '"Yah, yer father's in prison!" she hissed spitefully' (p.106)	the girls, from well-off families, are snobs – it's not the Kelveys' fault that *they* are poor Lena is being deliberately cruel to the Kelveys – she is angry that Lil doesn't react to being taunted

     See if you can make up to *five* further entries on your chart.

   b) Use your notes to talk **as a class** about how Katherine Mansfield makes you feel *sympathy* for the Kelveys. You might consider:

- the way she describes their appearance

- what she tells you about their family background

- the way she makes the other girls speak to, and about, the Kelveys

- how she pictures Lil and 'our Else' at the end of the story.

c) **By yourself**, write briefly about the way in which Katherine Mansfield tries to arouse your sympathy for the Kelveys in the paragraph on page 103 beginning 'They were the daughters of a spry, hard-working little washerwoman . . .'. In the course of your writing, say whose *viewpoint* you think she is presenting in each of these sentences:

- 'Very nice company for other people's children!' (page 103)

- 'It was impossible not to laugh' (page 103)

- 'The Kelveys never failed to understand each other' (page 104)

2 **As a class**, re-read i) the opening paragraph of *Through the Tunnel,* and ii) the ending of the story, from 'In a short while, Jerry swam to the shore . . .' to 'It was no longer of the least importance to go to the bay' (pages 120–1).

Talk about the part played by the opening and the ending in the story as a whole. You might consider:

- Jerry's feelings in the opening paragraph, about the 'wild and rocky bay'

- what the opening shows about Jerry's relationship with his mother, and hers with him

- Jerry's attitude towards the bay at the end of the story, and why he holds it

- Jerry's relationship with his mother by the end: has it altered during the story?

3 In the course of *Through the Tunnel*, Jerry's feelings about *himself* develop and change.

a) **In small groups**, trace these changes and the sequence in which they happen. Make an enlarged copy of the grid below for each of you. Discuss the quotations in the left-hand column (they follow the order of the story), referring to the full text to help you.

Say what each quotation **i)** shows about Jerry's feelings at the point where it occurs and **ii)** tells the reader about the changes Jerry goes through from start to finish. Write what you decide in the right-hand column of your own grid.

Quotations	Your own comments
1 'He swam back to shore, relieved at being sure she was there, but all at once very lonely' (p.111)	
2 'But he was happy. He was with them.' (p.111)	
3 'He cried openly, fists in his eyes' (p.113)	
4 'He knew he must find his way through that cave, or hole, or tunnel, and out the other side' (p.115)	
5 'It was not his beach.' (p.116)	
6 'If he did not do it now, he never would' (p.117)	
7 'He could see the local boys diving and playing half a mile away. He did not want them' (p.120)	

b) Then share your group's comments with the **whole class**.

End this discussion by considering why the story is called *Through the Tunnel* – and whether you think the title is a suitable one.

4 Writers sometimes use *symbols* to help get across a message in their stories. Symbols represent ideas, or themes, that are important to the writer.

As a class, talk about stories you know – especially fairy-tales, myths and legends – in which symbols are used. Start by considering what could be represented in a story by:

- a dark, dense forest without pathways

- a grinning skull

- a rose surrounded by thorns

- the face of a clock with no hands.

Then discuss what might be represented in *The Doll's House* and *Through the Tunnel* by the following symbols:

The Doll's House	*Through the Tunnel*
• the Burnells' courtyard	• the 'wild and rocky bay'
• the inside of the doll's house	• the 'safe beach'
• the 'little lamp'.	• the 'cave, or hole, or tunnel'.

Mysteries

The Angel of the Central Line **by Nina Bawden**

The Bewitched Jacket **by Dino Buzzati**

1 There are a number of similarities between *The Angel of the Central Line* and a dream. For example: the narrator's nightmare-like experience in the Underground, the settings, the other characters, the mood and the atmosphere of the story.

In small groups, take turns to re-read the story aloud from 'There was a train waiting' (page 123) to 'I breathed in exhaust fumes and tasted the lovely smell of real life' (page 127). Try to get into your reading a suitable pace and tone for what is being described.

Discuss and note down any features of the writing in this section that have a dream-like quality. It will help your discussion if you refer to some of your *own* dreams and compare them with the details of the story.

Now re-read the ending, where the narrator tells her grandmother what happened to her. At any point after she escapes from the Underground she *could* have written:

'Then I woke up, and it was all a dream.'

Say whether you think the actual ending is a better way of 'rounding off' than just saying that – or whether it leaves you, as a reader, feeling let down.

2 In the section of *The Angel of the Central Line* describing the narrator's tube journey, a strong *atmosphere* is established.

a) **As a class**, discuss the following passages in order to see **i)** what *kind* of atmosphere each of them creates and **ii)** exactly *how* it does so.

- 'It was freezing outside, ice underfoot and vicious needles of sleet slashing into my face. I kept my head down, slipping and slithering, but I managed to stay upright.' (page 123)

- 'Bank was a huge underground station, miles of dim, leaking tunnels and crumbling spiral stairs.' (page 123)

- 'I went on, hauling myself up the stairs, hand over hand on the rail, fighting against the flood of people, the raging tide.' (page 124)

- 'I heard the distant rattle-bang-roar of the approaching train. Then its lights flashing yellow in the dark of the tunnel, then the swish and the rumble as it drew into the station. And stopped.' (page 125)

In the course of your discussion, your teacher should help you comment on the writer's use of **i)** adjectives **ii)** verbs and **iii)** adverbials to create particular effects. Make notes on what is said.

b) **By yourself**, write *one* paragraph for the opening of a Mystery Story in which you describe either someone who is totally lost in dangerous surroundings or someone running through an unfamiliar place to escape from a pursuer.

Use writing techniques similar to those you have looked at above to make your paragraph as dramatic and atmospheric as possible. You can decide for yourself whether to write in the first or the third person.

3 There are a number of similarities between *The Bewitched Jacket* and a traditional fairy-tale.

As a class, examine these similarities. As you talk, fill in your own copy of the circle-grams opposite to show what the main similarities are. Where you find differences, note these down too.

l

Typical ingredients of a traditional fairy-tale	Features of *The Bewitched Jacket*

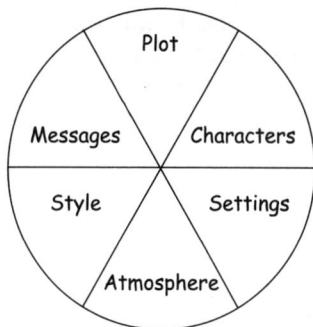

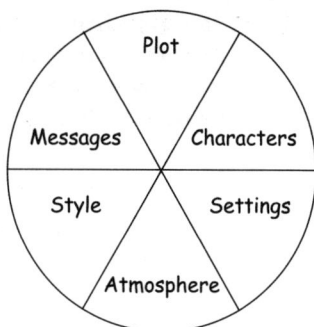

Plot

Messages   Characters

Style   Settings

Atmosphere

Plot

Messages   Characters

Style   Settings

Atmosphere

How successful do you think Dino Buzzati has been in adapting a traditional genre to hold the interest of modern readers?

4 **By yourself**, re-read the ending of *The Bewitched Jacket* – the section beginning 'By car I arrived at a secluded valley in the Alps' (page 134). It is written in the first person, by the narrator who is also the story's central character.

Re-write this section using the *third person*, from the viewpoint of a detached narrator. You can alter some details of description, but keep to the main outline of the plot.

As a class, read aloud several of your third-person versions. Discuss how effective they are. Then compare them with the original. Has changing the narrative viewpoint made any major difference to the impact of the story on a reader? If so, how?

5 *The Angel of the Central Line* and *The Bewitched Jacket* are both Mystery Stories. They are, however, told in different ways and with different purposes.

a) **In small groups**, discuss which of them you think is more effective in creating a feeling of mystery. Which story do you feel would make the better film? Why?

b) **As a class**, share the ideas you came up with in your group discussions. Then draw up several writing frames. **By yourself**, use one of these to create your own Mystery Story.

And Finally . . .

The Secret Life of Walter Mitty by James Thurber

1 Walter Mitty is one of the great daydreamers in literature. This story is based on two parallel journeys Walter Mitty makes: a 'real life' journey through New York and a 'daydream' journey through his own imagination.

   a) **In small groups**, work out how the story is constructed by making a labelled diagram of Walter Mitty's two journeys. Do it like this:

Walter Mitty's 'real life' journey

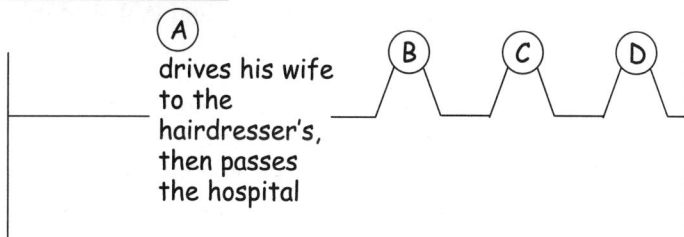

(A) drives his wife to the hairdresser's, then passes the hospital   (B)   (C)   (D)

Walter Mitty's 'daydream' journey

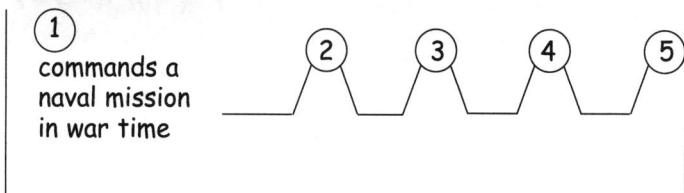

(1) commands a naval mission in war time   (2)   (3)   (4)   (5)

At each 'stopping point' on his daydream journey,
Walter Mitty imagines himself to be a different hero-
figure. Discuss and note down what *kind* of hero he
sees himself as at points (1) – (5).

In the course of the story, there are a number of
'triggers' which either jolt Walter Mitty out of a
daydream or springboard him into another one.
Find these triggers. Note them down, then add
brief explanations of how they form *links* between
his real and his imagined experience.

b) **As a class**, share your findings. Talk about how the
writer has planned out his story in *sections* and how
effectively you think he has done this – are there, for
example, any weak 'links'?

2 The main way James Thurber creates the character of
Walter Mitty is by using *contrast.*

a) **In pairs**, find examples of the character contrasts
between Walter Mitty as he really is and Walter Mitty
as he would like to be. Evidence of the former comes
from his conversations with his wife, the policeman,
the parking-lot attendant, and the A and P shop
assistant. Evidence of the latter comes from
conversations he has with people in his daydreams.

Explore the contrasts between 'the two Walter Mittys'
by filling in an enlarged version of this grid:

Character qualities of Walter Mitty in his real life	Character qualities of Walter Mitty in his secret life
1 a downtrodden, weak man who's treated like a child by Mrs Mitty (p.137)	a fearless and decisive leader of men who all hero-worship him (p.136)
2	

When you have finished, join up with another pair. Compare grids. Add to yours any points made by the other pair which you agree with, but haven't included.

b) **By yourself**, write an account of *Walter Mitty: the Man and the Myth*. Make a copy of your grid to help you:

- bring out his 'two' characters clearly

- explain the writing techniques James Thurber uses to give a picture of them both.

3 In each of the 'daydream' sections, James Thurber imitates the style of a different narrative genre.

a) **As a class**, read aloud each of sections ① – ⑤.
– or go into small groups and tape-record two or three sections of your choice.

b) **As a class**, make notes for a class poster about **i)** the events **ii)** the characters **iii)** the settings and **iv)** the dialogue in each section. Relate these to the particular genre James Thurber is imitating there.

Divide your class poster into four columns. Each column should be headed with the name of one genre included in the story – War Story, Crime Story, etc. Enter in each column the typical features of these genres which you noted down during class discussion.

4 **By yourself**, choose *two* of the sections ① – ⑤.
Re-write each in a different genre from that used by James Thurber. You can choose genres that Thurber ignores – e.g. Romance, Ghost Stories, Science Fiction, Westerns, Mystery Stories, etc.

You will need to adapt the events and the characters to fit the genres you select. Be as flexible about this as you wish – but make sure you feature a Walter Mitty 'hero' character, which can be yourself.

Suggested Further Reading (pre-1914)

The stories listed below were all published before 1914. They are either part of the English Literary Heritage or are drawn from Other Cultures and Traditions.

You may enjoy them in their own right – or may wish to compare them with some of the stories in this book. Many of them are printed in other **New Windmill** volumes (see page 183).

Relationships

Tony Kytes, the Arch-Deceiver	Thomas Hardy
The Gift of the Magi	O Henry
Désirée's Baby	Kate Chopin
The Poor Relation's Story	Charles Dickens
The Grasshopper	Anton Chekhov
The Nightingale and the Rose	Oscar Wilde

Crimes

The Adventures of Sherlock Holmes	Arthur Conan Doyle
The Tell-Tale Heart	Edgar Allan Poe
The Devil	Guy de Maupassant
The Stolen Bacillus	H G Wells
The $1,000,000 Bank Raid	Mark Twain
My Favourite Murder	Ambrose Bierce

Ghosts

The Red Room	H G Wells
The Signalman	Charles Dickens
The Hanged Man's Bride	Charles Dickens
The Masque of the Red Death	Edgar Allan Poe
The Transferred Ghost	Frank Stanton
The Duel	Guy de Maupassant

Science Fictions

Manuscript found in a Bottle	Edgar Allan Poe
The Balloon-Hoax	Edgar Allan Poe
The Man Who Could Work Miracles	H G Wells
The Time Machine	H G Wells
The War of the Worlds	H G Wells
Dr Jekyll and Mr Hyde	Robert Louis Stevenson

Childhoods

The Son's Veto	Thomas Hardy
The Half-Brothers	Elizabeth Gaskell
The Ransom of Red Chief	O Henry
Country Living	Guy de Maupassant
Dream Life and Real Life	Olive Schreiner
His New Mittens	Stephen Crane

Mysteries

The Magic Shop	H G Wells
The Withered Arm	Thomas Hardy
The Fall of the House of Usher	Edgar Allan Poe
The Haunted House	Charles Dickens
The Green Door	O Henry
The Queen of Spades	Alexander Pushkin

Other New Windmill Short Story Collections

The following collections include stories listed on pages 181–182. A full listing of each volume's contents can be found in the **New Windmills** catalogue.

Mystery Stories of the Nineteenth Century
Myths, Murders and Mysteries
Nineteenth Century Short Stories
Sherlock Holmes Short Stories
Stories from Different Genres
Stories from Other Times
Stories from Two Centuries
Stories Then and Now
The Withered Arm and other Wessex Tales

You might also enjoy the following **New Windmill** collections of short stories:

Don't Make Me Laugh – The New Windmill Book of Humorous Stories
Fast and Curious – A New Windmill Book of Short Stories
Just in Time – Short Stories from Ten Leading Children's Authors
Taking Off! – A New Windmill Book of Fiction and Non-Fiction
Tales with a Twist – A New Windmill Book of Short Stories
Trouble in Two Centuries – A New Windmill Book of Short Stories
Words Last Forever – Short Stories by Malorie Blackman

![Heinemann logo] **Heinemann**
New Windmills

Founding Editors: Anne and Ian Serraillier

Chinua Achebe Things Fall Apart
David Almond Skellig
Maya Angelou I Know Why the Caged Bird Sings
Margaret Atwood The Handmaid's Tale
Jane Austen Pride and Prejudice
J G Ballard Empire of the Sun
Stan Barstow Joby; A Kind of Loving
Nina Bawden Carrie's War; Devil by the Sea; Kept in the Dark; The Finding; Humbug
Lesley Beake A Cageful of Butterflies
Malorie Blackman Tell Me No Lies; Words Last Forever
Ray Bradbury The Golden Apples of the Sun; The Illustrated Man
Betsy Byars The Midnight Fox; The Pinballs; The Not-Just-Anybody Family; The Eighteenth Emergency
Victor Canning The Runaways
Jane Leslie Conly Racso and the Rats of NIMH
Susan Cooper King of Shadows
Robert Cormier We All Fall Down; Heroes
Roald Dahl Danny, The Champion of the World; The Wonderful Story of Henry Sugar; George's Marvellous Medicine; The BFG; The Witches; Boy; Going Solo; Matilda; My Year
Anita Desai The Village by the Sea
Charles Dickens A Christmas Carol; Great Expectations; Hard Times; Oliver Twist; A Charles Dickens Selection
Berlie Doherty Granny was a Buffer Girl; Street Child
Roddy Doyle Paddy Clarke Ha Ha Ha
Anne Fine The Granny Project
Jamila Gavin The Wheel of Surya
Graham Greene The Third Man and The Fallen Idol; Brighton Rock
Thomas Hardy The Withered Arm and Other Wessex Tales
L P Hartley The Go-Between
Ernest Hemmingway The Old Man and the Sea; A Farewell to Arms
Barry Hines A Kestrel For A Knave
Nigel Hinton Getting Free; Buddy; Buddy's Song; Out of the Darkness
Anne Holm I Am David
Janni Howker Badger on the Barge; The Nature of the Beast; Martin Farrell

Pete Johnson The Protectors
Jennifer Johnston Shadows on Our Skin
Geraldine Kaye Comfort Herself
Daniel Keyes Flowers for Algernon
Dick King-Smith The Sheep-Pig
Elizabeth Laird Red Sky in the Morning; Kiss the Dust
D H Lawrence The Fox and The Virgin and the Gypsy; Selected Tales
George Layton The Swap
Harper Lee To Kill a Mockingbird
C Day Lewis The Otterbury Incident
Joan Lingard Across the Barricades; The File on Fraulein Berg
Penelope Lively The Ghost of Thomas Kempe
Jack London The Call of the Wild; White Fang
Bernard MacLaverty Cal; The Best of Bernard Mac Laverty
James Vance Marshall Walkabout
Ian McEwan The Daydreamer; A Child in Time
Michael Morpurgo My Friend Walter; The Wreck of the Zanzibar;
The War of Jenkins' Ear; Why the Whales Came; Arthur, High King
of Britain; Kensuke's Kingdom; Hereabout Hill
Beverley Naidoo No Turning Back
Bill Naughton The Goalkeeper's Revenge
New Windmill A Charles Dickens Selection
New Windmill Book of Classic Short Stories
New Windmill Book of Fiction and Non-fiction: Taking Off!
New Windmill Book of Haunting Tales
New Windmill Book of Humorous Stories: Don't Make Me Laugh
New Windmill Book of Nineteenth Century Short Stories
New Windmill Book of Non-fiction: Get Real!
New Windmill Book of Non-fiction: Real Lives, Real Times
New Windmill Book of Scottish Short Stories
New Windmill Book of Short Stories: Fast and Curious
New Windmill Book of Short Stories: From Beginning to End
New Windmill Book of Short Stories: Into the Unknown
New Windmill Book of Short Stories: Tales with a Twist
New Windmill Book of Short Stories: Trouble in Two Centuries
New Windmill Book of Short Stories: Ways with Words
New Windmill Book of Short Stories by Women
New Windmill Book of Stories from many Cultures and Traditions:
Fifty-Fifty Tutti-Frutti Chocolate-Chip
New Windmill Book of Stories from Many Genres: Myths, Murders
and Mysteries

How many have you read?